ANAL COUSINS

ANAL COUSINS

Case Studies in Variant Sexual Practices

by

WILLIAM MALTESE

The Borgo Press
An Imprint of Wildside Press

MMVII

CONTENTS

INTRODUCTION

"I JUST ABOUT HAD my cock on target at the opening of her snatch when she slapped my pecker away; damn, did that sting.

"'Wait a minute, boy,' she said. She was calling *me* boy. That made me so goddamned mad. She was younger than I was and was treating me like a fucking child. Truth of the matter, as regards sex, she probably *was* a lot more knowledgeable about it than I, even now, am.

"'What do you mean, *wait?*'

"'I invited you here to plug my ass, not my cunt, buster. Now, either do *that* or fuck off.'

"She reached around her upturned ass, grabbed hold of my dork, without a by-your-leave, and stuffed the head of it right into the crease between her buns.

"'Like fuck *this* hole,' she said. She jiggled her little ass until my cock sat the opening of her anus.

"'You want your ass fucked, baby?' I asked her. 'Well you had just better prepare yourself for one hell of a butt-humping. Because, as God is my witness, that is just what you are going to get, right here and now.'

"So, I started pushing my meat into her.

"'For Christ's sake,' she squealed. 'Try being a *bit* careful. The rate you're going, you're going to split me wide open. And if you don't think I'm going to tell your mother if and when that happens, you are sadly mistaken.'

"So, I pushed a *little* slower.

"'Jesus, you are dumb,' she said. 'Lather that prick of yours up with a little spit, why don't you?'

"So, I spit in my hand and cocooned my dick with my saliva. Then, I again worked my cockhead, slippery this time, into her rectum and shoved. My prick started, once again, to slip in, albeit more easily this time.

"'Now, you're talking, baby,' she whimpered. 'Now, you are *finally* starting to get the idea.'

"I pushed in a couple inches. Her ass was the tightest thing I had ever fucked. The only time I had ever even had a near-similar feeling was the time I cut a too-small hole in a cantaloupe I screwed in a hot summer field. The pleasure resulting from this submersion up cousin-butt was so enjoyable as to be actually painful.

"I kept shoving and shoving. She kept wiggling and wiggling her little ass, working it so that more of my inches slipped right inside.

"Apparently, though, I wasn't moving fast enough for her, any longer. Just the opposite— apparently, I now moved too goddamned slow.

"'Get *all* of your big dick on in there, you bastard!' she commanded. 'I want to really feel it. Push, push, fucking push!'

"So, I pushed harder. I arched my pelvis and brought it back down to ram a couple more inches of my dick up her ass. She groaned and wiggled her butt again.

"'More!' she squealed.

"So, I fed her more of my stiff meat. She was so tight that every inch of me into her was like ramming through a knothole two sizes too small. The shaft of my cock bowed under the exertion.

"Then, suddenly, her rear passage just seemed to open wide and let me slide the rest of the way, like a train gliding nonstop through a tunnel. My lower belly suddenly whacked her upturned ass, and my balls banged against her upturned backside.

"I don't know how she could have ever taken all of me. I mean, I am *really* big. Some girls have complained when I jabbed all of my peter up their snatches. But this time, I actually had all of me up a hole that didn't have its owner complaining. Eve took each and every inch of me. What's more, she loved each and every inch she had, too.

"'Fuck me, baby! And fuck me good! I fucking love it!'

"Unfortunately, I wasn't quite used to anything quite as tight as her ass. The pleasure was almost too much even before I started actually to pump. I just gritted my teeth and tried to prevent my climax from coming. But there was no way I could have stemmed those tides, so I didn't.

"My nuts let loose their creamy load with frantic cannon-shots that shook me from my head to my toes.

"After which, I realized Eve was laughing.

"'You are just a baby boy,' she said. 'You can't even hold off like a man.'

"Jesus, when she said that, I swore to God that my cock wasn't about to go soft just because I'd already blasted one load. I knew, too, that there was more than a good chance of my making good on that promise. There had been times when I had masturbated three times in a row before my old pecker finally started losing its starch.

"Well, when my dick stayed hard, and I started humping her asshole for sloppy seconds, that broad had a different tune to sing. It wasn't more than three seconds before she was back to grunting like the stuck pig she was and enjoying every damned minute of it.

"She babbled like crazy, moaned, and uttered all sorts of gibberish that I couldn't understand. After I had fucked her steadily for a solid five minutes, I noticed that her eyes had gone all glassy, and her mouth was drooling spit.

"I had reached a point where I didn't give a damn whether I ripped her wide open. This broad had my cock up her ass and, more importantly, was going to know it was there, doing what it was doing. I could always tell my parents that Eve had gotten me so hot and bothered that I couldn't help myself. After that talk I'd had with the old man, just a few days previously, I figured my parents would be quick enough to believe the very worst I could say about Eve.

"I watched my cousin's face for a long time and then centered my attention on her boobs. Those two jelly-like masses were just shaking like sixty on her ribcage. They were really something to see, let me tell you. I mean, they were really sweet-Jesus whoppers.

"Then, I looked farther—all of the way to her snatch. And since I was pretty limber from gymnastics at school, I decided to try something on Eve that I hadn't tried on any other girl. I decided this was my opportunity to see how good I was at eating out pussy. So, still with my big cock up her tight asshole, I just bent my head down and affixed my mouth to the pouty lips of her snatch.

"I'd heard a lot of guy-talk about eating pussy. I'd heard how it was *really* what the dames liked. One guy told me that once you'd tongued a bitch she was yours for life.

"So, while my cock fucked Eve's bunghole, my tongue fucked her twat. And, Jesus, did that girl ever go bongos! She started making all sorts of loud noises that were even more animalistic than the ones she'd been making before.

"I just buried my old tongue so deeply down her cunt that I thought I might actually touch China. Then, her hands were clawing away in my hair. At first, I thought she was trying to pull my head away. But she was actually trying to shove my face down even closer.

"And, yes, just like I heard it would be, her pussy smelled like fish, and it had a decidedly oily taste to it. None of which really did all that much *for me,* but it was really turning *her* on. And I wanted her to get turned on a whole lot. I wanted her to realize that this skinny, pimply-faced kid could give her the kind of butt fuck and cunt-gobble that she'd never had before and would be hard-pressed to get again.

"In about ten minutes, because of the extreme tightness of her asshole, I was on the verge of yet another nuts-rumble. I went back to trying to hold off my inevitable explosion. My cock and its cock-head just kept ballooning, bigger and bigger, inside her with each and every stroke I gave.

"I pulled my face away from her cunt, tired of the taste and the smell.

"'No, please, keep eating,' she protested and moaned.

"But I didn't give a shit whether *she* wanted more of anything. In fact, I figured to leave her wanting more. I figured to have her wanting me back for *mucho* repeats, once this particular session was over.

"I really started to concentrate on royally pumping her ass. My cock's juice puddled inside her and made her anal pit as lubricated as it could be.

"I slipped my hands under her ass to heave her even farther up and over my erection.

"Then, the tempo of my fucking went into genuinely high gear. No doubt, I was fast approaching *my* point of no return. I just turned into a human piston. I started puffing, panting, and gasping for breath. My body turned sweaty and wet with perspiration.

"Eve screamed and shouted, off into yet another climax. If I'd counted right, give or take a couple, that bitch climaxed about five times after my dick slid up her tight asshole.

"While my cock continued working, Eve started finger-fucking her snatch. Every time I'd heave my prick up her rectum, she'd jab her hand deep up her pussy. A few times, my cock actually felt her fingers working away inside her vagina. That was really wild. It was like she was masturbating me with her hand at the same time I was fucking her bunghole; hell, maybe that *was* what was happening.

"Our fucking bodies made all kinds of wet sounds.

"We were one machine out to achieve one purpose: mutual orgasm.

"I couldn't hold back. I had this tremendous desire to really blast up her butt. I bucked on top of her a few more times and, then, splattered her climax-spasming anal cavity with another steamy load of my hot spunk."

* * * * * * *

THE ABOVE EXCERPT, from one of the following case histories, is an example of two sexual deviations that—even in times of the greatest sexual permissiveness—are still looked upon by the majority of society with abject horror: anal sex and incest.

Dr. Georges Valensin, in his *Sex from A to Z*, states:

> Incest is not biologically unnatural. Animals, except for certain pigs, have no aversion to it. Its prohibition is moral, and even when it was permitted, as in ancient Egypt and Persia, it was reserved for the ruling families. The most common form of incest is between father and daughter. It is still frequent in France, in rural areas and alcoholic families. Next comes brother-

sister incest. Mother-son incest and homosexual incest are much rarer.

In preparing any body of case studies, it is always impossible—due to mere space limitations—to provide a completely comprehensive glimpse into any psycho-sexual subject. The next best thing is to attempt to find a good cross section, and that's what I've tried to do in ***Anal Cousins***.

A thorough check of countless case histories, plus many personal interviews with potential subjects, has led me to the following examples of anal sex between first cousins.

It will be seen by the reader that such sex does not necessarily limit itself to any specific level on the social scale. It occurs among our country's landed gentry as well as in the slums of our cities. Nor is there specifically one major reason why cousins commit incest of an anal nature. Although as Robert Goldenson states in *The Encyclopedia of Human Behavior*:

> It has been found that incestuous relationships occur most frequently where...opportunities for sexual experimentation constantly present themselves.

In this book:

Case One tells of Carolyne and her two cousins, Rodney and Kenny, and provides an example of how the need to maintain vaginal virginity can lead to anal sex before marriage.

Case Two is Adam's story (of which this book has already provided a brief preview) and which details his relationship with his cousin, Eve, a young lady so used to penile manipulation of her vagina that anal sex is necessary to give her the satisfaction *normal* sex can no longer provide.

Case Three is an example of how traumatic experiences—in this instance multiple rapes—can turn a woman to anal sex.

Case Four details a homosexual relationship between two male cousins, one of whom is more anal-oriented because of voyeuristic incidents experienced early in life.

* * * * * * *

Incest is nothing new to society. The apparent fear of it is nothing new, either. The fear has been passed down from the earliest times. However, it is not the purpose of this research to label any of the people presented herein as perverted. The perversions of today are, after all, the norms of another day.

Barbara Bross and Jay Gilbey, in their *Complete Sexual Fulfillment*, state:

> Incest has sometimes been deemed perversion. It is not. It is a social taboo. It becomes a perversion only in so far as it may leap a generation and put partners of widely differing ages together.

The cases in **Anal Cousins** are not as unique for their incestuous nature as they are because of the sexual directions taken within these incestuous relationships. All four cases are those of cousins who primarily engage in sex with an *anal* orientation.

Anal sex, like incest, is probably as old as time itself. Mention of it has been made in books and pictures of almost every culture. It has long been known that there were sexual pleasures derived from manipulation of the anal canal. Each of us, in childhood, was faced with the realization that our rectum was an erogenous zone.

From *The Encyclopedia of Human Behavior*:

> [Anal-erotic] sensations arise in infancy during the anal phase of psychosexual development when the child derives gratification from expulsion, retention, or observation of the feces. If the libido or pleasure drive is arrested or fixated at that stage, the individual will have a tendency to derive special pleasure from this region in later life.

This eroticism does not necessarily disappear as one grows to maturity, either. Inge Hegeler and Sten Hegeler say in their *ABZ of Love*:

> The area round the anus is not only generously provided with nerves, but...it is furthermore connected with the sexual organs by means of muscle fibers, and...this area can therefore be

of great sexual importance to some people.

James Leslie McCary, in his book *Human Sexuality*, says:

> The perineum of both man and woman is sensitive to manipulation. This area includes the anus and inner portions of the thighs, and extends from the anus to the lower region of the sexual organs. About half of all men and women, in fact, report that they experience erotic reactions to some sort of anal stimulation.

The following comes from *Complete Sexual Fulfillment*:

> There can be no doubt that the anus is a genuine erogenous zone of the body in men and women. The nerves that line the anal opening and lead back from it are nerves that produce erotic sensations. Therefore, the anus is a legitimate organ of sexual pleasure.
>
> Generally women are found to be more anal-erotic; some prefer stimulation of this area to vaginal stimulation. If a wife is honestly anal erotic, she should let her husband know about it, for this is quite common.

There is some indication that the horror surrounding anal sex may finally be beginning to abate. Mention of it as a successful means of sex is being seen in more and more non-fiction and fiction books that are popular with the masses.

The pseudonymous author "J," writing in *The Sensuous Woman*, states:

> For rectal intercourse—the most comfortable position is for you to lie on your stomach with your hips elevated by one or two pillows. Your partner will apply surgical jelly or Vaseline generously to his penis and your anus and then slowly and gently enter you fully…. After he has entered you completely, the man will slowly begin an in-and-out stroke and treat your anus as if it were your vagina. Once you have let your sphincter muscle relax, you will find yourself enjoying some quite remarkable sensations, and if you encourage your partner to play with your clitoris while he is making anal love to you, you are capable of having quite an orgasm.

I.

THE FARMER'S DAUGHTER

"**I COME FROM A VERY LONG LINE** of prudish and very strict farm people. Now, I don't know what that means to you, but to me it means that the pigs, horses, chickens, and cows can fuck from sunrise until sunset; the hired help can play around and bunghole each other after the day's work is done; the married people can keep those old bed springs squeaking way into the night; but, little Carolyne was going to stay a virgin until the right man came along to rip her hymen.

"Unfortunately for me, I had one of those hymens that was there to stay unless some hard cock battered it down, or some doctor removed it surgically.

"My mother was as proud as all hell that any husband of mine was almost assured of finding that particular piece of skin to rupture. When I first started dating, she'd come into my bedroom after I got home just to stick her finger up my cunt to be sure I was still virgin. Can you imagine that?

"I used to go horseback riding all of the time in hopes that I'd tear the fucking thing loose. But no luck. The day I married John, his cock couldn't even rip the damn thing, it was in there so solidly. I had to go to the doctor after all.

"But you're not interested in my marriage to John, are you? You want to hear about me and my cousins, Rodney and Kenny.

"Well, my cousin Rodney, I can tell you, was really something. The two of us had one hell of a time while it lasted. Jesus, but I can still get hot just thinking of those times Rodney and I had together.

"If my mother and father, not to mention my husband, John, only knew what kind of a virgin I *really* was at the time of my marriage, all sorts of shit would likely have hit the fan.

"I don't know when I really started paying attention to Rodney. Sexual-type attention, I mean. We were together a lot during our childhood. His home was just over a small rise. All our relatives were just over the next rise or in the next little valley. My great-grandfather used to own all the land. When he died, he left sections of it to his favorite kin for them to build houses on. Everyone worked together to make the combined farm and cattle lands pay off. At the end of each year, all the profits were divided equally.

"So, it's really kind of hard to say just when I had my sexual awakening. Just one day, there it was. And the first thing I remember was seeing that ridge of meat running cousin Rodney's left thigh. At the time, he was pitching hay into the loft. He had his shirt off. Jesus, he had a body. And he had the cock to go with it. I remember once hearing one of the farm hands joking about how Rodney had shoved his wrist-thick tool up *some cow's asshole.*

20

I've yet to see a bull that had a dong bigger than Rodney.

"Anyway, once the mood struck the both of us to get together, there was plenty of opportunity. There was an awfully lot of land around there owned by the family. There was an awfully lot of little private places where two young kids could get together to do a bit of sexual exploration.

"I suppose the both of us were really a tad over-sexed. Rodney sure as hell was. Whenever he knew I was watching him, he'd work at that ridge of his crotch with one or both of his hands. Neither of us thought too much about the fact that we were *first* cousins, either. At that age, the sex thing was a lot more powerful than taboo blood connections. Anyway, it wasn't like the two of us were brother and sister. If anything, that we were related only added to the excitement of the sex thing.

"The first time we ever did anything sexual was at the swimming hole. There were a lot of swimming holes on the farm, but this one was kind of out of the way. The farm hands always swam one closer to home. We had to walk our horses up this narrow little path that went up the mountain. It was really too much bother if all you had in mind was just a swim.

"I followed Rodney there one day. Though I pretended to be sneaky, I really knew damned good and well that he knew I was following. When I finally got there, he was already stripped down and in the water. I kept concealed and just watched him. It was really exciting. The water made it really impossible to see much of anything, but that only let my imagination run away with me.

"He must have been playing with himself in the water, because his cock wasn't shriveled up at all when he came on out to dry himself. That was really the first time I actually saw his prick free of his pants. You could have heard my gasp a mile away. Jesus, but that hunk of sausage was really something to see.

"Right then and there, my little cunty just started leaking like sixty. And about that time, Rodney took his cue and started playing with himself.

"He started some serious fiddling with his whanger that made it swell bigger than it already was. He wrapped both hands around its circumference and started caressing.

"The damned thing just kept getting bigger and bigger and bigger. It was huge, then huger, and then hugest. When the fucking thing was fully erect, standing up straight with its red head reared way passed his belly button, I could hardly breath I was so turned on. Then, the bastard, still using both hands, started pumping.

"Then, when I was panting so goddamned hard and fast from watching, he got this big-ass grin on his face. He looked up to where I was hiding behind the rocks.

"'Get your little ass down here, cousin Carolyne, and take a look at a man really close up.' That's what he said. He knew I'd been there all along.

"So, I came down for a closer look. All the time, he kept on beating on his meat. Jesus, it was all I could do to say anything. I just stared, fascinated by his swollen hunk of manhood and the way his hands kept working it. Then, he started revolving his hips sensuously and literally fucking his fists.

"'You like the looks of that, cousin Carolyne? Do you, huh?'

"'Jesus, Rodney, put on your pants. If anyone besides me sees you out here, doing that, you'll get your ass tanned to within an inch of your life.'

"He laughed. He knew, as well as I did, that he wasn't going to put his britches back on, not for a while anyways. He also knew that I didn't want him to put on his pants, anymore than *he* wanted to put them on.

"'Let's do *it*, cousin Carolyne. What do you say? No one's ever going to find out.'

"'Do *what?*'

"'I want to fuck you, that's what,' he said. About that time, I had juice running down the insides of my legs.

"'No way,' I told him. I could tell, just by looking at his cock, that once it started into my cunt, there would be no way in hell my hymen would stand up to the attack.

"'Come on, gal. You put out for the other guys, why not for your cuz?'

"'You nasty-minded, horny, bastard, I haven't put out for shit. And if you think I'm letting that pipe of yours rip my hymen, so my old lady can give me hell, you're full of it.'

"'As if your old lady would ever know,' he said; he laughed. Then, the expression on his face changed. 'Then again, knowing old mom, I'll bet she *does* check.'

"But Rodney wasn't giving up yet. He started whipping his dick even harder.

"'Look at this cock of mine, Carolyne, honey. Just look at it. It's all big and solid and just all hard to pop cum into your snatch. You won't regret saying yes to it, baby. It and I promise you one hell of a fine fuck. Come on. Try us; you'll like us.'

"By that time, he was really flogging his old hog. And my snatch was leaking so goddamned much that I thought for sure he'd see the damp spot oozing my panties and jeans.

"And you know, right then and there, I actually, almost, gave in to him. I actually, almost, let my legs flop open to take that monster cock of his. I was so hot, I was almost dying. His eyes were getting all glassy. His body was all slick and shiny with sweat.

"'Come on, cousin Carolyne. Please?'

"'I can't, Rodney. My old lady would find out for sure. Really, she would.'

"'Then, let me fuck you in the ass, honey. How about I do that?'

"Jesus, I don't know what happened, then. Suddenly, he just grabbed me and started yanking off my clothes. And rather than fight him, I helped him. For some odd reason, the idea of his sticking his prick up my ass really got me excited.

"His cock was so red and swollen. It just kept banging against his belly. The huge slit that gashed its top was leaking clear juice. Every time that thick head hit his stomach, it splattered new wetness all over the place.

"When I was naked, he rolled me onto my belly on the grass. Then, he sat across the back of my thighs, kneading my buttocks. He grasped the mounds of my butt between his fingers. Finally, he stuck one of his fingers up my warm and clinging asshole. My anal muscles protested the intrusion, spasming as he probed my hole deeper. Finally, though, my sphincter relaxed, and his messing with my bung *really* felt good.

"He pulled his finger from my pit and leaned forward. The tip of his slime-covered penis nudged my rear door. His prick oozed even more sticky goo that ran the crease of my ass.

"Then, he really leaned his cock into my butt, and the first of those lovely inches of his slid home. He pressed harder yet, giving me more and more of his pecker.

"I cried out, surprised that I was getting as much pleasure as I was from being on the receiving end of an ass-fuck. My whole body trembled with the enjoyment of his entering tool. Before he was even in all the way, though, he started pulling out. He withdrew his prick out to its tip, and then shoved in me again. He did this a few times and then, finally, jammed his penis all of the way: from its tip to his balls.

"I squealed with the sudden agony and pain. My body twisted beneath his. Automatically, my ass reacted by heaving upward. This did nothing but lodge him even more firmly within me. Any pleasure I had had from the lead-in was suddenly gone completely. There was only the pain, the torment. There was only the flashing heat—red-hot— spasming through me. I felt hit by lightning.

"I mumbled and cried in pain. But my sounds and thrashing beneath him only seemed to spur his passions. He really began pumping my asshole, all the time keeping me pinned beneath him with his hard body. He fucked and fucked and fucked. His inches frantically slipped and slid my bunghole. The thickness of his dick raised all holy hell with my virgin butt. And it seemed as if his cock just, impossibly, kept ballooning larger and larger. I thought any minute his dick would literally explode and blow my guts to kingdom-come along with it.

"Each lunge of his huge prick made my anal walls stretch to their limits. I actually thought I wasn't going to be able to stand it. I actually thought I was going to die.

"And then the pleasure began to return. Though my ass still ached with the movement of his hard cock within it, it was suddenly a different kind of ache—an almost *pleasurable* ache, if you know what I mean.

"Rodney's lower belly ground my upturned mounds. His penis pressed my warm and clinging inner bowel. The momentum of his humping increased. His fuck-strokes became shorter, more rabbit-like.

"He slobbered all over my shoulders. His hands worked beneath me, his fingers pressing and squeezing my already bruised tits. He moaned and groaned, like an animal. He bit my shoulder and, as if in direct result, his hips went into pumping fast-gear.

"His prick pistoned in and out, in and out, so goddamned fast that I couldn't even count each thrust and withdrawal.

"I climaxed. Can you believe that? I actually shook and shuddered orgasm all over the damned place. I could hardly believe it. I mean, there was nothing rammed up my cunt. No cock, no finger, no tongue, nothing. And yet my insides were going ape-shit. I came, and my whole body shook with the pleasure of his thick manhood working away at my asshole.

"As a result, my anal muscles really started working over his dick. They gave that pipe of his such a fucking massage that Rodney wasn't long in blasting his guts, either.

"He blasted and blasted to fill up my asshole with his spunk as well as with his big dick. He gave me so much of his thick and creamy jism that its combined mess overflowed, ran the crease of my butt, and cum-painted the insides of my thighs.

"Still, he kept pumping me: gone wild. I was a bucking bronco and he was my cowboy rider. He was screaming and shouting, groaning and moaning. I felt more and more of his hot cummy explosions exiting his prick and trying to find a place to set down in my already filled-to-capacity butt-tube.

"His hips banged continuously into my ass, his meat moving back and forth inside me, his balls shooting more and more of his thick cream up me and mine. Finally, his hips dropped onto me one final time, his total inches totally rammed deeply inside me.

"He pressed his sweaty chest and belly into my back and ass, his mouth against my ear.

"'That was one hell of a bung-fuck ride, cousin-of-mine, Carolyne,' he said.

"And I had to agree with him. It was.

"Then, he did something that really surprised me. It was something that would continue to surprise me, whenever he did it, even later on, after we'd done this sort of thing for a long, long time.

He waited a couple of minutes, and he started to hump my ass again. He didn't even go soft after his first blasting.

"'What are you doing?' I asked. Wasn't that the silliest damned question ever? It was obvious what in the hell he was doing. That thick old prong of his was again working my ass. His spent cum still flooding my butt was all the lubricant his cock needed for continued easy sliding.

"My anal muscles again began tightening around his submerged prick. He hefted out about four of his thick inches and proceeded to plow them right back in. His prick took on an even greater hardness, pressing firmly against the tender membranes lining my asshole.

"He moved his dork in and out, his belly again smashing my ass cheeks.

"'Jesus,' I muttered, 'I'm ripping this time, for sure!'

"But at that point, I really didn't care whether I was ripping or not. I only knew that there was the pleasure, and that the pleasure was the direct result of his fat cock's continuing prod of the hole between my buns.

"He pumped my butt frantically. His prick made decidedly funny noises as it non-stop churned the stale sperm slopping the inner corridors of my asshole. He pressed his hips to drive his prick into the furthest recesses of my body. Every powerful surge he provided made my butt shudder and stretch.

"His lower body rose and fell, his cock rubbing sensuously inside me. His balls dragged along my buns, climbed upward to the base of his dick where they would remain until they blasted out their next thick ocean of steamy spunk.

"'Jesus, I'm close, again, *already*,' he groaned into my ear.

"He was obviously trying his best to slow down his momentum, in order to prolong the fuck. He even managed for a moment, but only for a moment.

"His blond pubic hair mashed the curving mounds of my ass.

"I groaned with the maddening pleasure. My squeals vaguely resembled those of a stuck pig.

"He wrapped his arms about me, each hand cupping one of my tits as his hips continued to work his prong within me. He paced this thrusts and withdrawals, and tried desperately to control the passions that must have been rife within him.

"The ending strokes of his fuck were long and fast. His penis throbbed even before it started shooting its latest barrage of sticky cream.

"I went off before he did. The surge of which filled my belly and sunburst outward to stiffen all of my muscles. About this time, Rodney bit my ear. In my passion, I bit my lip and tasted my blood.

"His hands slid from my tits, working down between my belly and the ground. His fingers found and played with the lips of my cunt.

"My ass thrust upward and met his body, grinding my ass into his pubic bush at the base of his dong.

"'Jesus Christ, I'm coming, baby! It's now!' he bellowed.

"His whole body went rigid on top of me. He jiggled on me, shaking with such violence that his cock almost slipped completely from my ass. Then, he collapsed on top of me, grinding my body into the ground as his prick dove one final time to its full limits.

"His penis discharged in a series of spasmodic eruptions that flushed my butt with his seed in a volume that closely rivaled the load he'd splashed there before it.

"He moaned and groaned. Then, he quit moaning *and* groaning; he even quit moving. I would have thought him dead if not for his heavy breathing.

"Actually, I thought (hoped) he was resting up for a third assault on my anus. But his cock—finally—started going soft inside me.

"He pulled his hips upward, dragging his limping pecker behind him. When his dick pulled free, it made a funny sucking-like noise. I thought it sounded like a cow pulling its leg out of the mud.

"The withdrawal of his dong brought with it more fluid to trail my ass crack.

"I just lay there, exhausted beyond belief. There was a dull ache in my ass.

"Rodney started licking my spine. When he reached the small of my back, his hands pushed apart my buns. Only this time, it wasn't his cock he put inside me; it was his tongue.

"For some reason, don't ask me why, tongue-fucking seemed *dirty*, and I tried to roll away.

"'No, Rodney. Not that.'

"'Yes, baby. I want to. Really, I do. I want to suck your sweet ass dry of my cum.'

"Before I could say anything else, his nose and his tongue were shot between my buns, snorting and licking up the stale semen that clung to the crease and within the doorway of my asshole.

"It was an experience that was entirely different from cock down there.

"His tongue was long, but it wasn't as long as his dick, and it certainly wasn't as hard. It was just really one hell of a strange sensation, the way it was rolled prick-like and jabbing away at my butt hole.

"Okay, it was really wild having his tongue flicking back and forth inside me. And it really worked me over. I mean, it *really* worked it over. Fucking licked me clean! It was everywhere: up and down my crack, licking, licking, licking.

"He pushed my buns even wider, and placed his puckered lips right over my anal opening. With all his following sucking and blowing, I went ape-shit.

"I climaxed again, my body shaking.

"I was all wet and exhausted. The tongue-fuck orgasm left me limp as a dishrag. But Rodney didn't care. He kept right on doing what he was doing. His nose snorted, his tongue licked, his lips kissed away.

"When his tongue wasn't up my butt, when his nose wasn't nuzzled against my rectum, his finger probed.

"When he was finally finished, he rolled me onto my back, and lowered himself down on top of me. His chest pressed my sweaty titties. His belly was hard against mine. His cock was against my snatch. But I didn't have to worry about his prick suddenly out to plug my virgin cunt in a surprise attack. His dong was limp as they come and curled like dead venom-less snake between us.

"He put his face really close to mine. He smoothed the damp hair out of my eyes.

"'Did you like what your little cousin's big cock did for you, honey?' he asked.

"And what could I say to that, I ask you? I wrapped my hands round his neck, pulled his head down and kissed him full on the lips, tasting me and tasting him and enjoying the all of it.

"'Honey,' I said. 'Anytime you want to fuck my butt, you just give a hillbilly yell.'

"He said, 'How about I do *just that,* first sign of sunup tomorrow?'"

* * * * * * *

CAROLYNE AND RODNEY have one thing in common with the other subjects in these case studies: they fully realize the incestuous nature of their affair but are in no way hindered by it.

It's very interesting that while many of the subjects interviewed would not, by their own admittance, participate in a father-daughter, or mother-son incestuous relationship, cousin-cousin seems so far removed from the general consensus of "wrong-doing" as to offer hardly any obstacle if any. The fact that it is an act of incest being committed might even be extra enticement, if the truth were know.

Says Dr. Georges Valensin in *Sex from A to Z*:

> ...although the practice of incest is exceptional, desire for it one time or another is the rule, according to scrutinizers of the unconscious.

One of the prime factors leading to Carolyne and Rodney's incestuous affair can be traced to

Carolyne's parents' insistence that she maintain her virgin status until marriage. During one of the several interviews with Carolyne, she revealed that her mother, upon marriage, was *not* a virgin, and her husband (Carolyne's father) really never let his wife live that fact down: often raving during family arguments that his wife was "used merchandise" when he'd married her.

The following quote is from Dr. Albert Ellis's *Sex Without Guilt*:

> Assuming that human beings who remain virginal till marriage are more pure and saintly than those who do not, the thesis cannot very well be upheld that they are commonly happier and more joyful. To fornicate may be 'sinful'; but it is also a rare delight. Perhaps we would be saner to work at making it less rare rather than less delightful.

As it was found quite early in Carolyne's life—through a number of routine physical examinations—the girl's hymen was of the type that would probably necessitate surgical removal. Her mother utilized this as a check on her daughter's sexual experiences. As a matter of fact, as indicated, Carolyne's mother waited up for her daughter's return from dates and actually inserted her fingers up Carolyne's vagina to determine if the hymen was still intact.

Says John Warren Wells in his *Comparative Sex Techniques*:

> ...older women may play a role in the child's (sex) learning process. The daughters of the upper classes, especially in England and France, were frequently taught to masturbate by nursemaids who handled the girl's genitals until sexual excitement resulted; later, the girls would imitate the nursemaids' actions and masturbate themselves.

In Carolyne's instance, as the extreme strength of her hymen disallowed complete penetration of her vaginal cavity, the young woman often experienced incomplete orgasms, even via self-masturbation and, likewise, experienced the resulting frustrations that resulted from such dissatisfaction.

Examination leads to the conjecture that the demand put on Carolyne, by her mother, to retain virginal status, is one of those instances indicated by Dr. Albert Ellis in his *Sex Without Guilt*:

> Virginity, especially when it is prolonged and taken to extremes, seems to be the true enemy of love (and often engenders deep-seated hostility to others). Sex without love, moreover, is hardly a heinous crime, and appears to be quite delightful and to add immeasurably to the lives of literally millions of individuals.

It is quite apparent, even to a novice, why anal sex becomes such an important aspect of Carolyne's relationship with Rodney. The girl needs sexual fulfillment. Seeing how natural intercourse is out of the question, she chooses anal intercourse as a logical alternative.

Say Louis P. Thorpe and Barney Katz in *The Psychology of Abnormal Behavior*:

> A child frequently develops anxiety when his normal needs for sexual expression come into conflict with the standards of behavior set for him by parents. It is the conflict between the desire for sexual activity and the opposing forces of the child's social and moral training that generates the anxiety....

* * * * * * *

"I'LL TELL YOU, WE DID OTHER THINGS, too, besides corn-holing.

"I guess we did them just to see if we could find anything better. In the long run, however, we usually ended up with his fucking my ass. We both got more pleasure out of that that out of anything else we tried.

"Once I decided I'd try to give him a blow job. He was conveniently resting on his back. I crawled on my hands and knees, up and over him. His giant cock was aimed along his muscular belly. I hovered over the damned thing, letting my eyes take it all in. I let my gaze travel from the tip of that baby right on down to where it was anchored at his stomach near those huge blond-haired balls of his.

"I pushed my hands under his ass for support.

"Even though his eyes were shut, he must have suspected what I was planning, because he heaved his hips up so that I could work my hands really far under him for better leverage.

"I lowered my head down over his cock and sucked up the tip of it. I let it slide in as far as I could without choking. He put his hands on my head, trying to shove me down over him even further. For a while there, I thought I was going to gag to death on his huge piece of raw sausage.

"God, he had one big pecker, if you know what I mean. It was almost impossible to get the whole thing into my mouth, let alone down my throat.

"Jesus, did he ever start getting excited, though, with the feel of my lips running his cock shaft. He groaned and demanded me to, 'Suck it. Suck it'. Then, he started to say things, like, 'Lick it like a lollipop, baby!'

"He bucked his hips like crazy and, as a direct result, I took even more of his thick inches down my gullet.

"About that time, I decided that sucking cock might be okay for the guy, but it sure isn't anything great for the one whose lips are wrapping the dick. The more I sucked on his old peter, the more *he* seemed to like it, though. But it still wasn't doing too much for me.

"I grabbed one of his hairy balls. My fingers closed in about the base of his cock. I ran my fingers through his pile of wiry pubic hair.

"'Great, baby. Just great,' he said, with even more accompanying moans and groans.

"His cock grew bigger in my mouth. Each time I gave another suck of it, it did seem a little easier to take.

"I stuck my tongue into the slit at the end of his pecker, and that boy must have thought he was in Seventh Heaven. As far as I was concerned, on the other hand, none of this cock-in-mouth business was anything to write home about. And the taste of him was a bit—well—too damned salty to tell the whole damned truth of it.

"He still had his hands on my head. Every opportunity, he pushed my face down over his dork so that my nose nestled in his pubic hair. He smelled all sweaty.

"Those times I managed to pull away as far as the tip of his goddamned cockhead, he'd immediately push me down over his full dick-length again.

"I didn't get too much of a charge in looking at his cock, up close, either. It was really ugly with all its blue veins running its thick shaft. His balls were big and round as golf balls. His nuts had hair all over their containing bag. Up close and personal, his scrotum looked like a couple of prunes grown together and gone all wrinkly and hair-grown.

"Well, I kept on sucking, good sport that I was. When he really started moaning in this quaking full voice, I really went to town on that joystick of his. Frankly, I was suddenly just trying to get the fucking ordeal over with as quickly as possible. I really didn't know too much about sucking cock, then. As a matter of fact, his was the first peter I'd gone down on. It, therefore took me longer than it would today to—finally, finally, finally—get his nuts off.

"I just knelt there between his legs, with his cock and sometimes even his balls in my mouth. I tongued his prick all over the place, even jabbing in between his pecker's gashed lips. I sucked, sucked, and sucked some more, trying to get that cream out of his balls so that we could get on to something that was just a bit more pleasurable for me.

"Just when I thought I was going to have to give up and leave him without an exploded boner, his cock started—thank God!—gushing. It wasn't cum, though. Nothing creamy and thick. It was pre-cum; the kind his cock leaked all of the damned time. Sometimes, because of it, he didn't even have to use spit when he fucked my asshole. All he had to do was milk his cock and all this fluid came out that he could spread over his dork, like icing over a phallic cake. Great for ass-fucking; for eating—Naw!

"I kept on eating penis sandwich, though, and he kept on squirming until, finally, I figured enough was enough. I said to myself: *'Fuck this'*. My throat ached, my lips were bruised, and I was tired of even the possibility that I might choke to death on his nasty-getting-nastier schlong.

"The next chance I got, I yanked my head completely free of his lap, letting his old dong just flap—*thwack!* —back against his belly. I heard this disappointed groan coming out of him, and I dodged his hands when they reached for my head in order to make me go down over him again.

"'Please, baby,' he said through a loud moan of disappointment. He *did* sound downright pathetic and needy. 'Jesus, don't stop there.'

"'Listen,' I told him. 'None of this is any too damned exciting for me. You want your cock sucked, *you* go right ahead and suck it.'

"He got the idea. I guess he decided that I wasn't kidding, because the first thing I knew, I was on my back, on the ground, and he was lifting my legs. I was afraid he was going to lunge for my pussy by way of revenge, so I put my hand protectively over my snatch. But he had long ago learned that I wasn't going to let him in there. By that time in our relationship, he probably liked putting it to my ass better anyway.

"He bucked downward and forward. When his dick slid my asshole, I just relaxed and let the bulk of it glide on in. He groaned as he buried it. He lifted my legs even higher so that they wrapped his neck. I locked my ankles behind his head and squeezed my asshole tightly down around his pecker.

"He started working his dick inside me. He worked it in and out, and then he revolved his hips so that his pisser stirred up my asshole. I was getting this exciting feeling inside me. His hands started roaming all over me. They finally came to rest on my jugs. He started playing with my nipples until they went taut as thumb tacks.

"His big prick just kept on ramming in and out of my butt. His hands kept on squeezing my titties until my whole body was on fire. I felt strangely tingly from head to toe, and my snatch was leaking like crazy.

"I started panting, and I could see that his body was really getting sweaty. Trails of liquid ran his forehead and along the sides of his nose. He was *really* moaning and groaning. My sucking had got him genuinely worked up to begin with. Now, his just-sucked cock submerged up my asshole, his nuts weren't too damned far from cracking.

"I shut my eyes, and I let the pleasure start to take even more a hold of me. He was going to blast pretty soon, and I wanted to get *my* bennies off, right along with him.

"Every time he shoved his prick up me full depth, my body responded to it as if his dick provided a bona-fide electric shock. I started wiggling my ass to stir his pecker up my butt hole all the more.

"I could feel my orgasm building at one and the same time as Rodney's fucking took on greater momentum. If I weren't careful, he was going to let loose his creamy load and leave me wanting. Of course, there was always the good chance that he would screw my ass a second time, after he had blasted his first, but there was sure as hell no point in my counting on that if I didn't have to.

"So, I started really banging myself over his dick. I rammed my ass into his pelvis, and ground my buns around the root of his thick prick. He got busy on my boobs. His fingers dug into my tit-flesh as if he were a baker working dough. And my nipples went so fucking hard that I thought they were going to pop right off my jugs.

"Then, he started bellowing. His body started tensing. He was right there, good and ready to blast his wad.

"About that time, I didn't care whether he blasted or not. I was feeling that damned good. I took his each and every additional fuck-stroke as icing on the cake.

"Then, he gave this one big final lunge that put him up me from his cockhead to his pelvic bone. I reached for his primed cum-bulged balls and squeezed as hard as I could.

"With the feel of his hot gushing cream inside me, I blasted way off into the universe. It was really wild and exciting.

"I gave his balls another good squeeze. He screamed and, by the way he screamed, let me know that he wasn't feeling any real pain.

"It was always just a sex *thing* between Rodney and me, did I mention? He was great during a butt-fuck, with his nice body and his big whanger, but while I loved his cock up my butt, and he loved it there, we were never *in* love. When you're *in* love, you're willing to give and take a little. I mean, I don't mind blowing the sizable cock of my husband, someone I care for. When you love someone and wrap your mouth around his dick, there's real joy in doing that, but no real joy happened for me when I was eating Rodney's pecker; so, there was never a second sucking of his cock, at least by me.

"I'm glad I did eat his dick that once, though, especially at the time, because I was hot to experience as much different sex as I could, short of vaginal penetration. It was an exploratory period in my life, and eating Rodney's dick was just one more bit of exploration, although it was one that didn't warrant repeating.

"Rodney and I used to meet all the time for sex. Oh, he didn't devote all of his fucking time to me. He got into some of the cunt to be had from his classmates. But he kept coming on back to me regularly for a piece of the rear action.

"Then, somehow, Kenny, Rodney's older brother, found out that Rodney and I were doing it. I think Rodney must have let it slip, probably bragging and all. Anyway, Kenny starts showing up at my house whenever Rodney is off somewhere else. Kenny starts mooning around and making wise-ass remarks, like, 'If you want a real man, I don't know what you're doing hanging around with my know-nothing brother; I'm the one in the family who has the know-how.' At first, I just ignored him, pretending I didn't know what the hell he was talking about.

"Then, one day, he cornered me down in the barn.

"'How about letting *me* corn-hole you, honey?' he said. 'Why should my horny little brother have all of the fun working your ass?'

"I asked him just who the fuck he thought he was. I, also, told him if he didn't quit talking dirty, I'd tell my mother and father. So, he asked me just what I thought my ma and pa would say were they to discover that I'd been letting Rodney, my very own cousin, plug my asshole. He said the least I could do was share a little of my stink hole with him. After all, he was my cousin, too. And, he added, 'I even have a bigger dick than my brother.'

"Well, I really wasn't all that enthused. If I gave in to Kenny, there was liable soon to be a long line of other cousins come around and expecting me to go belly-down in the grass for them, too. Rodney and Kenny were both good-looking studs but, Jesus,

I had a mess of relatives whose faces would have sunk ships.

"As it ended up, Kenny grabbed my hand and shoved it between his legs.

"'Feel *that* hot-for-you monster-pecker, why don't you, baby? It's just a dying to hot-poke itself up your ass. Not kiddy pecker, mind you, but real man-meat.'

"Christ, it *was* as big as a loaf of bread. Anyway, it sure as hell *felt* that way through his jeans, against my fingers. Actually, I thought he'd stuffed his pants with something to fool me. I started squeezing the length of it, trying to determine just how real that piece of meat was—if it was real meat at all. As I was playing with it, it started extending even further down his leg.

"'You want to shove *that* up my asshole?' I asked him.

"'Come on, honey. I've shoved it up a lot of assholes in my time. I just thought it would be kind of nice, since we're cousins, if you'd put out a little for me as well as for my numb-nuts brother. Even though he's boasted that you've got one very-very-very tight bunghole—' And didn't *that* just spill the beans as to *whom* had gotten himself one major case of diarrhea mouth too many? '—I'm sure you can safely take on this big sausage of mine, since I promise I'll plug you real nice and easy.'

"Well, with all that talk about Kenny jabbing his hunk of monster-meat up my butt, I got turned on. My cunty started dripping juice, like a leaky faucet dripping water; it seemed damned weird to me, at the time, how my cunt took to spasming at my having just a thought of hard dick getting rammed up its companion sex-hole.

"'So, pull out that hunk of meat of yours and let's see just how big it *really* is,' I told him. 'Then, we'll just see whether I take it on or not.'

"I stepped away a little, and he unbuttoned his jeans. He pulled out his whanger. I remember, he wasn't wearing any underdrawers. He kind of laughed and hoisted out his big balls to join his dick in the fresh air.

"Jesus, if Rodney had a piece of meat, *and he did,* his brother's cock put Rodney's pecker to holy shame. Kenny's prick was the Jolly Green Giant of pricks, in comparison to most male sexual equipment I've seen to this very day. Of course, I hadn't really seen that many cocks, back then, so it looked exceptionally impressive. I should have expected it to be, though. There had been jokes going around the family and around the school about the size of his sausage for as long as I could remember. I just hadn't paid all that much attention to them before I'd became genuinely interested in dick.

"I took one look at that thing of his and told him I doubted very much whether I was going to let something that big even *try* getting up my tight ass. Taking on Rodney's monster was one thing, but taking on Kenny's telephone-pole dick was bound to get my ass ripped from stem to stern.

"He only laughed and assured me that it wouldn't hurt. 'As a matter of fact,' he said and silly-ass grinned, 'it's going to feel really good for the both of us.'

"By that time, I was so excited that I was more than willing to take a chance to see just what it would feel like. If Rodney's cock was able to get my jollies off, what could a cock like the one had by Kenny's do for me?

"He was all hot to roll me on my belly and give it to me that way. However, I had enough experience with Rodney to know that once a guy got on top of you, you didn't have too much say about how he pumped it to you. Kenny was probably the type to get so goddamned hot and bothered that he'd thrust it into me, without a by your leave, whether my butt started ripping or not.

"I told him I'd give his Paul-Bunyan dick a try on one condition: he had to get down on his back and let me take my own sweet time sitting on him. He wasn't too happy with that variation, but his cock was so hot to trot that he wasn't about to say no.

"He wanted us to strip down stark naked, but I wasn't too hip on that idea, either. The barn was one place where almost anyone could walk in and catch us, but we were both so goddamned hot to trot, we weren't about to go looking for a safer place. I told him we'd go up in the loft and leave our clothes *on*. Then, if anyone came in, we wouldn't have too much adjusting to do.

"So, he went up, first, and lay down in the hay; his cock and balls still poked through the gape in the crotch of his jeans.

"I followed him and lifted my dress, took off my panties and buried the latter in the hay. I was just lucky to have worn a dress that day. Had I been planning on going horse-back riding, instead of monster-cock riding, I would have worn my jeans.

"I squatted down over him, his cock beneath me like some giant log toppled in some forest. I reached down a hand and felt his massive woody for real, for the very first time; it was like a heat-hardened rubber hose. I tugged it up so that its fist-like head aimed toward my ass and the rafters. I rubbed the tip of his already-juice-leaking dickhead back and forth along the crease of my butt.

"His pre-cum clung to the valley between my buns.

"Right away, he starts groaning and moaning and telling me to hurry it up and sit my ass on down.

"I teased him a bit more, first, though, still not sure that I was going to go through with it. For the moment, I just let the head of his pecker rub against the puckered access to my little asshole. I wiggled my hips so that the very end of his dork could press on through. That felt so goddamned good that, momentarily prepared to follow his urging, I commenced one *very slow* sit-down.

"More of his cock pushed on through. Jesus, it was big. For a while, I was thinking that I wasn't going to be able to take it. I mean, my asshole kept getting wider and wider. After his cockhead and a couple of his lead cock-inches got in, I didn't see how my ass walls could be stretched any further.

"His prick was smallest at its tip. After that, its shaft flared and kept on doing so until halfway down when it, only then, started its minor taper to its thick root. It looked rather like a cobra if you know what I mean. The further toward mid-shaft I slid, the more my asshole had to stretch.

"But after a few jiggles over those few first inches buried in me, I got so goddamned hot that I knew I was going to end up taking all of them, even if my ass ended up torn from here to California.

"It was suddenly so exciting to have all of his meat on its way inside me when, up until then, I'd figured cousin Rodney's cock would be the biggest I'd ever be able to take.

"I just kept sitting, sitting, sitting, and he started bucking his hips up and down, up and down, up and down in an attempt to bury even more of him inside me.

"His prick must have really been leaking like sixty up my hole, must have really been lubricating my anal corridor, because my slide over his pole just got easier and easier. I was really surprised at just *how* easily his dick was going in, just how fast it was disappearing up my clutching a-hole.

"Finally, my ass actually touched down on his muscular belly. I jiggled a little bit more to let every last available fraction of his big prick adjust up my butt.

"My sphincter gummed shut, rubber-band tight, about the base of his butt-plugged erection.

"I was facing so I could see his face. His eyes were closed, his mouth was open, and his tongue was hanging out like one of a dog in heat.

"I grabbed his hip bones and used them for supports. I began to pull my ass up around his shaft. I lifted really slowly until only the head of his dick was left inside me. Then, I sat down *really* fast, my hole gulping his dick up to its root in one massive swallow. Then, I started moving atop him, up and down, up and down.

"He squirmed with pleasure. It was exciting for me to see *and feel.* I'd rise way up, and his hips would follow in order to keep his cock inside me for as long as possible. Then, when his ass collapsed back into the hay, I'd follow after, my butt gobbling up his thick pecker for one more time. I was really giving that thing of his one hell of a wicked ride.

"My guts started churning, because I was really turned on by Kenny's face all twisted up with my good-time merry-go-round riding of his big dick. His lips opened and shut, and his tongue darted in and out to wet his lips. His chest ballooned with all his gasping. His throat gargled little whimpering sounds.

"I just kept right on bouncing, feeling his dick traveling my anal passage.

"I twisted my butt on his dong, waiting for him to scream out his pleasure (which he did) and bring a whole bunch of concerned people running from the house (which he didn't). Kenny was no dummy. He knew that if he made any *really* loud ride-me-to-climax sounds, his fun would be ruined, and he likely wouldn't get more. So, he kept on biting off his each and every intended scream.

"All of a sudden, his cock was shooting wad after sticky wad of hot, thick, cum up my asshole. And this girl was in Seventh Heaven.

"The minute I felt that slime draping my insides, I started bouncing up and down on his spitting rod like crazy. And Kenny went wild. I thought for sure that he, at any minute, was going to let out a *'Haaaaw-Hoooooh!'* to bring each and every one within miles to watch the ongoing action.

"My ass rocked over his erection and kept right on rocking even after his cock was through blasting.

"I knew his dick, if it was anything like that of his brother, was going to be so climax-sensitive, after blasting, that it would really feel the painful pleasure of my continued humping over it. And once I started my own orgasm, there was no way I could have stopped my jiggling ass, over his spent prick, anyway.

"He grabbed my thighs and did try to stop me. But honey, there was no way on God's green earth he could have prevented my seemingly non-stop dance of pleasure.

"When I was finished, he was almost crying from the pleasure/pain I'd put him through. My heaving over his pecker hadn't allowed his dick to go even partly soft, even though it had blasted and had wanted to do a bit of natural shrinking.

"'You hot-assed little bitch,' he said, and it was almost an accusation. But he wasn't *really* complaining. We'd both enjoyed one hell of a fuck, and we both knew it.

"After that first taste I had of Kenny's cock, I kind of lost interest in Rodney's big-but-smaller dick. Every time I could, I'd put off Rodney and make a bee-line to Kenny. After awhile, Rodney good-naturedly accepted that I'd pretty much cut him off, completely, in favor of his brother. Oh, I didn't keep my ass from him entirely. Sometimes when he begged really hard and nice, or really looked like he was going to go wild if he didn't stick his cock somewhere, I took pity on him and gave in. But those times became fewer and farther between.

"So, I suppose I'm kind of responsible for sending him off to get one of his *let-me-fuck-your-pussy* girls knocked up. Her name was Mary, and he actually ended up marrying her. Even after he did marry Mary, though, that didn't stop him from coming round to me, looking for an occasional piece of ass, and I do mean *ass*. Sometimes I even let him have it.

"Then, I guess, he got tired of his wife *and* me, because he enlisted in the Army and went off to basic training. After which, I was able to devote full time to Kenny. And Kenny could sure come up with some weird things for us to do.

"One time; he took me out to the barn where this young calf was still young enough to be nursing. Kenny pulls down his pants, goes over to this calf, and start's shaking big Kenny-dong right in the little fellow's face. The calf must have thought it was one hell of a tempting teat being offered it, by way of a meal source, because it opened its mouth and closed right in on and over it. His furry little head just nuzzled right up tight against and actually butted Kenny's lower belly.

"I stood there, just watching for the longest time; then Kenny said, 'Hey, babe, why don't you see if *you* can think of something to do to join in.'

Always happy to oblige, I knelt behind Kenny and pried open his butt cheeks. I had a close-up view of his pucker responding to his fucking motions. Every time his hips pushed his dick into that calf's face, Kenny's little asshole winked shut. Every time his hips pulled his dong out, his little pucker kind of puckered.

"I decided to stick my finger up his ass to see what his anal muscles, way deep inside, were up to. I spit all over my middle finger, getting it all nice

50

and wet. Then, I shoved it up his butt and immediately started working it there.

"I found this little walnut-size prostate and started prodding it with my fingertip. Kenny told me that he really liked to have me 'tickle his prostate.' I didn't know too much about prostates, then. For that matter, I still don't. All I knew and know is that it really gets men excited when I play with it, as if it's the equivalent of a woman's clit.

"I gave my finger a couple more twists and turns in his butt. My free hand reached around between his legs and started massaging his balls. Then, he turned his head back over his shoulder, looked down at me and said, 'Come on, baby, French kiss my asshole.'

"I wasn't really too hip on kissing his ass, or anyone else's, but I thought I'd give it a try. As I've mentioned, those were still my experimental days, and how could I expect to find out about things if I didn't give them a try at least once?

"So, I pulled my finger out of his hole in preparation for substituting my mouth there. I spread wider the buns of his butt to check out his pucker more closely. It winked at me. It was so damned cute; I didn't waste any more time in placing a big juicy kiss right smack dab on it.

"'Jesus, Jesus, Jesus,' Kenny said and kept on saying over and over.

"He was really having one hell of a time, no doubt about it, his prick up that clammy calf's mouth, his ass sucked by yours truly.

"My face was up against his asshole as close as I could get it. My tongue was up that tight and funky male rear corridor of his with a vim and vigor that surprised even me.

"His pucker relaxed for more of my hearty tongue-fucking. I pushed in as far as I could go. His hole tasted of something, but *of what*? It wasn't really unpleasant, as far as tastes go, but it wasn't genuinely yummy, either. I also remember his ass smelled of shit *and* Lifebuoy soap.

"My tongue rolled into a slick little prick and really started fucking man-slit. If, as with cock-sucking, tongue-fucking wasn't doing a whole hell of a lot *for me,* Kenny (like his cousin when I'd swung on Rodney's dick), was really having a good time.

"I finally lost complete interest, however, in any additional tonguing of his ass. So, I pulled out and went back to ramming my finger up there. With my finger again battling his prostate, he probably got more jollies off than he did on my disinterested tongue anyway.

"It wasn't long before he really started moving his hips. Every time he pulled his cock away from the calf, my finger would disappear up his humping butt. I was just thinking about whether or not I could get another finger or two up his asshole when he interrupted my thoughts by blasting.

"He pushed his pelvis so that his prick was buried all the way down the calf's throat. By the way Kenny was groaning, he was giving that animal one healthy feeding of thick hot spunk.

"I pulled my finger out of his butt, and Kenny really yelped.

"The poor calf was undoubtedly expecting something far different than the cream he ended up with from Kenny's large and exploding pseudo-teat.

"When Kenny finally pulled out of the animal, my poor cousin was really all wiped out.

"He turned to me with this silly-ass expression of his. One last oozing of his cum dribbled from the head of his pecker and trailed all of the way to the ground before breaking.

"No doubt that Kenny really liked getting his joint sucked by that calf while I played with his prostate. After the calf got teeth, though, we quit having these little threesomes."

* * * * * * *

IT'S OF DEFINITE INTEREST to touch, however briefly, upon the aspects of bestiality which occurred in Carolyne's relationship with Kenny, if just because the distinct impression the subject gives is that it did occur with some frequency.

The action of bestiality when it doesn't interfere with normal intercourse is usually not considered as abhorrent by modern psychologists as some might think—especially as it is practiced with some frequency by youth, usually male, in rural areas.

State Thorpe and Katz:

> Bestiality...sometimes called zoophilia or zooerasty [is where] the deviate gains sexual gratification by engaging in sexual contact with an animal....
> In the United States, sexual contact

with animals is primarily engaged in by…boys in rural areas.

II.

ADAM AND EVE

"**HER** *NICKNAME* **WAS EVE.** That's kind of funny, because my name's Adam, as you very well know. That kind of makes our story like that story in the Bible, wouldn't you say? You know the one where Eve tempts Adam? Only this time, Adam wasn't quite so stupid to begin with. That's not to say that Eve didn't *think* I was stupid. For that matter, the ones who really thought I was a dummy were my parents.

"It's really amazing, sometimes, to see just how stupid parents think their kids are. I don't know, but I sometimes think parents believe we don't learn anything about sex until they tell us, or until we're married.

"It was really rather funny when I first found out that Eve was going to be living with us for a couple of weeks. By the way, I *should* say that her Christian name was Evelyn.

"Anyway, when it was decided that she was going to come spend sometime at our house—her father was dead and her mother had to go to the hospital for some *female* 'thing'—my father took me aside for one of those famous man-to-man talks every old man tries to have with his son at one time or another. Mother conveniently made herself scarce in the kitchen. I really wasn't too enthused about this talk shit. Dad and I had had several of them before then, and nothing had really ever come of any of them. As you very well know, by now, nothing much came of this one, either.

"It was really all quite ridiculous. He started out by saying some really silly-ass thing like, 'Son, I don't know how much you know about sex and all, or how that may apply to the troubles Eve has been having lately, but it would be better if you were not to get too close to her while she's here.' Then, he went through this great long speech on morals, even dropping the not-so-veiled hint that anything I did with Eve would be—ta-dah!—incestuous. You see, she *was* my first cousin.

"Eve had already been pregnant once. I guess she almost died when she and her boyfriend actually paid some local butcher (hey, I'm talking one of those real meat-cutter guys from whom you buy cutlets in the supermarket), to abort their baby.

"Eve was really supposed to be a wild kid. Members of my family were always talking about 'little' Eve's 'sexual exploits.' Of course, my old man didn't go into any great detail about *all of that*, nor how Eve was rumored to have had sex with every kid past puberty in her neighborhood. What he *did* say all boiled down to my needing to *watch out* for Eve, because she was a wild one and would corrupt simple little old me if given half the chance.

"You would have thought Eve was some professional whore who had seen it all—been there, done that, got the T-shirt, burned it, thrown away the ashes. In reality, she was only sixteen at the time. And confidentially, I found it a bit hard to believe, no matter what my dear dad said, that Eve's mother (her father dead in a fall on a construction site), had allowed her to go out and do all the shit she was rumored to have done.

"That said, I do see, in retrospect, that Eve's mother was something of a 'swinger' herself. After Uncle Paul died and left her a pile of insurance money, she might very well have been having too much of a good time to pay all that much attention to her daughter.

"When Eve's mother headed off to hospital, my father thought it was somehow *his* duty to step in and take care of her daughter. Maybe he was, himself, hot for Eve's pussy. That *could* be it, you know? I don't think I ever really thought about that possibility until now. Color me slow.

"Anyway, the old man gives me this little talk and tells me that we are only going to have to have this *bad seed* around for a couple of weeks. He certainly hopes that I'm man enough to stand up against temptation for at least that long. Jesus, but he's not to be believed.

"How in the hell is it that so many parents get hung up on this morality bullshit? Baby, if I wanted to fuck my own sister, and she wanted me to fuck her, believe to hell, we'd do the fucking. These older folks are straight from some Stone Age. They're especially uptight about this incest 'thing.' They're sure any kids resulting from such screws will be all wingey-dingey or something worse. They actually think we kids don't have a clue about contraception. Go figure!

"Anyway, Eve turned up at the house one day, looking a hell of a lot older *and better* than I remembered. And she came with quite a rack! I mean, that girl, at age sixteen, had tits you wouldn't believe. They just came bulging out to meet you, and you wanted to take hold and squeeze them by way of saying '*Hello*,' all the while wondering why the weight of them didn't have her toppling right on over from lack of balance. She had a slim waist, and a nice ass, too. She had cool good-looks with long blonde (and I do mean *naturally blonde*) hair.

"All it took was that one long-time-no-see look, even from an amateur like I, and I could tell just how it was that she just *might* have gotten into all the trouble she was supposed to have gotten into. Someone with the wow-factor she had certainly needed more than a swinging mother (in the hospital, no less) to keep her in tow. Two good parents would have been hard-pressed to keep a sweet babe, like she was, virgin for long.

"My parents put her up in the guest bedroom just down the hall from me. I don't know what in the hell they were thinking. First, they give me this big long line about how I should keep my distance; then they temptingly move her into a room not two doors away from me.

"When she came down for dinner that first night, she acted the perfect little lady. Confidentially, I think my parents were pleasantly surprised. God only knows what they had expected.

"Eve took one look at me, and I'm sure she thought I was just some poor little innocent clod who didn't know sex from finding babies under cabbage leaves. What else could she expect as the offspring of two parents like mine?

"Eve played it really cool. She knew she only had to bide her time for a couple of weeks until her old lady got out of the hospital. Then, she could get back into her groove again.

"When I first realized what a desirable perspective hump Eve really was, I suspect she hadn't even considered, for a moment, me as a potential sex partner. I was stick-thin, then. I had pimples.

"But that she was such a neat looking piece of ass, staying in the same house as I, really got my nuts stirred up. My dong, with its usual life of its own, just came bounding to full attention and stayed there. My loins got that pleasant ache they got whenever it was time to lock myself in the bathroom and jack off not once but five times in a row.

"I did a lot of masturbating in those days. And, although, my parents wouldn't have believed it, I also did a lot of fucking.

"I mean, hey, I might have had pimples on my face, and I might have been downright skinny but, baby, I had a cock on me that really made girls stand up (lie down) and take notice. When they wanted lots of male meat pumping away up their snatches, pushing them up to the skies with pleasure, they didn't give one fat damn what I otherwise looked like.

"I could easily wrap the length of my cock with both fists, one atop the other, and still have a good two inches of dick free at top *and* bottom. And that was when my penis was flaccid. It was so big that I used to get kidded, all of the time by guys jealous that their weenies were little-finger size in comparison. Those green-eyed-with-envy little pricks used to say, 'No girl is going to want something *that* grotesquely big shoved up her tight pussy!' Well, every one of those bastards has since had to eat his words.

"There were all sorts of girls who wanted my giant meat shoved inside them. And they weren't only in my class, either. I had senior babes who were hot to have me plow their guts on a regular basis.

"You can say anything you want to say about size *not* counting, but let me tell you, from experience, that a big whooper provides anyone who has it with lots and lots of bonus points. A broad sees a small pecker, and she thinks it's not up to doing what it's supposed to do. She may *say* something differently, she may even read all of the books that say differently but, down deep, she intuitively knows there's nothing quite like the stud who brings her and her pussy eleven-plus hard inches of plow-power.

"Now, when Eve first came to the house, she had no idea that I had such a big dick. She just saw a pimply-faced kid and didn't initially pay all that much attention.

"She didn't have to go to school while she was with us. I was damned jealous of that, too, don't you know. My parents wouldn't let *me* miss a day, but they'd decided it would be okay for Eve to be truant. After all, she remained officially enrolled in a school clear across town; for the short time she would be spending with us, it hardly seemed worth the time and effort to get her transferred.

"However, leaving Eve at the house was another of their big mistakes. My mother had her bridge club meeting every Wednesday, and dad worked every day but the weekends. So, that left little Evelyn all alone on Wednesdays. And who, but I, should happen to come down with a horrible headache at school one Wednesday?

"It didn't take too much effort to fake out the school nurse. I did, though, think there might be some difficulty when she said she'd call my house to see if it was okay with my parents if I left school early.

"Eve answers, and the nurse thinks that Eve is my mother and proceeds to tell her about my headache and my desire to come home. And, to my surprise (I fully admit it), Eve tells the nurse to go ahead and send me along.

"Jesus H. Christ, I realized that Eve was actually prepared to join me in my game, and my pecker really got hard. Suddenly, I worried that the nurse would see its impressive bulge extending right on down my pants leg.

"I ran all of the way home, as best I could with my boner like a splint against my leg. I arrived panting like a dog. I bolted into the living room, and there Eve was, sitting in a chair and looking at me with this cat-ate-the-canary expression.

"'You don't *look* to me like you have much of a headache,' she said. 'Just what bullshit were you feeding that teacher of yours?'

"Hell, my sexy cousin was younger than I was, and she acted like she knew it all.

"I told her *it* hurt like sixty (I referred to my cock, not my head), and I had to get relief for *it* fast. That was why I came home.

"She grinned, all know-it-all, and shook her head.

"'Listen here, honey,' she said. 'You feed all that bullshit you want to that little school nurse of yours, or to those no-nothing parents of yours, but don't try to unload even one shovel of it on me. I saw that *help-me-and help-my hard-cock* look of yours the minute you and your boner turned up early at the door.'

"She walked over to me and put her hand right on the swelling my dick was making in my pants. She squeezed.

"'See there,' she said 'It's all hard and ready and just waiting....'

"She let her fingers do the walking a little farther along my shaft, her mouth kind of hanging open in obvious surprise at the size of my still-growing pecker.

"'Jesus God in heaven! Is that all you, or do you have a lead pipe stuffed in your trousers?'

"I told her it was *all* me and, if she wanted a look, she could check out the real thing in living color. Also, I told her she wasn't the first girl to think that it wasn't the real McCoy, only to find out otherwise."

"She smiled at me, as if I were some little kid who didn't really know a hard-on from horseshit. Then, she lifted her skirt and dropped her panties— just like that. There was this twat of hers, all covered with sparse blonde hair, for my viewing pleasure. I almost started climbing the walls.

"'You're awfully slow in stripping down, aren't you, cousin?' she said. 'Or did you actually think I wasn't going to call your bluff?'

"She came closer and helped me undo my belt. I told her I could manage quite well without her assistance, and I took off my shirt, dropped my pants and underpants, and let my cock bound free.

"'Jesus H. Christ, it *is* real!' she exclaimed. She moved in for a closer look and took hold of it and squeezed. She then proceeded to milk it for some pre-seminal slime which she expertly (she'd obviously dealt with pre-cum before) spread like sugar syrup over the muffin-fat head of my dick.

"I almost blew right then and there. She was one of the few girls I knew who just walked right up and grabbed hold, no bones (except my boner) about it. Two thirds of the girls I knew before her didn't even care much about *seeing* 'it.' They just wanted it pulled out in the dark in order to *feel* it jabbed up their pussies.

"'Now that I see that piece of meat of yours, I just might actually give it a try,' she tells me.

"I was tempted to ram my cock up her invitingly hairy snatch, right then and there.

"'You do want to fuck me?' she said, as if I might be queer or crazy.

"My mouth fell open about three feet. Not because of the invite, but because *fuck* wasn't a word we actually spoke around our house. It was one of those words whispered only in the backyard or in the school locker room, or was scrawled on lavatory walls. No girl ever came right on out and asked.

"Well, Eve did. And she said it, again, squeezing my dong a little harder.

"'Sure as hell, I want to fuck you,' I told her. 'What in the hell do you think I told that lie about a headache to that school nurse?'

"Eve laughed as if I had just said the funniest thing in the world. Naturally, I asked her what was so funny.

"'*You* are,' she said. 'For acting like some know-it-all planned-for-this stud when I bet you really don't know shit from Sunday.'

"'You're in for one hell of a big surprise, baby, including my dick.'

"'You little innocent, you. I'll bet you haven't even screwed a girl's ass before.'

"'Ass?' Her ass was the last thing I would have suspected her or me wanting me to plug.

"'Yes, *ass*,' she said. 'I've been fucked up the cunt so many times; I don't even get much pleasure out of that same-o-same-o any more. What I'm looking for is a man who can give a good bung-fuck. Think you're that man, cuz?'

"Can you imagine all of that coming out of the mouth of a teenage girl?

"'You know what I'd *really* like,' she said. 'I'd really like the full length of that big dick of yours rammed all of the way inside my butt so far that I taste your pre-cum in the base of my throat.'

"It would be kind of hard to tell you just what I was thinking right then. All the broads I had fucked had never ever asked me to plug prick up their butts. As a matter of fact, on those few occasions when I had made the mistake, in the dark, of aligning my penis on some gal's rear entrance, you can't believe all the squawks of protest I heard. I was laboring under the impression, before that moment, that a girl's asshole was to be used for one thing and one thing only: shitting. Eve certainly took a very short time to set me straight.

"'Well?' she asked. 'Why don't you come on up to my bedroom and at least give it a try? And bring your shucked clothes in case your old man or old lady should bop in unexpectedly.'

"With that, she sashayed her ass up the stairs and into her room. I followed her like a little puppy on a leash.

"Once we got into her room, we proceeded to strip down completely. After that, she just fell on the bed and beckoned for me to come on down beside her. I still thought she was kidding about the ass-fuck business, so I stared to finger-fuck her cunt while I worked my cock for position to screw her sweet pussy.

"I just about had my cock on target at the opening of her snatch when she slapped my pecker away; damn, did that sting.

"'Wait a minute, boy,' she said. She was calling *me* boy. That made me so goddamned mad. She was younger than I was and was treating me like a fucking child. Truth of the matter, as regards sex, she probably *was* a lot more knowledgeable about it than I, even now, am.

"'What do you mean, *wait*?'

"'I invited you here to plug my ass, not my cunt, buster. Now, either do *that* or fuck off.'

"She reached around her upturned ass, grabbed hold of my dork, without a by-your-leave, and stuffed the head of it right into the crease between her buns.

"'Like fuck *this* hole,' she said. She jiggled her little ass until my cock sat the opening of her anus.

"'You want your ass fucked, baby?' I asked her. 'Well you had just better prepare yourself for one hell of a butt-humping. Because, as God is my witness, that is just what you are going to get, right here and now.'

"So, I started pushing my meat into her.

"'For Christ's sake,' she squealed. 'Try being a *bit* careful. The rate you're going, you're going to split me wide open. And if you don't think I'm going to tell your mother if and when that happens, you are sadly mistaken.'

"So, I pushed a *little* slower.

"'Jesus, you are dumb,' she said. 'Lather that prick of yours up with a little spit, why don't you?'

"So, I spit in my hand and cocooned my dick with my saliva. Then, I again worked my cockhead, slippery this time, into her rectum and shoved. My prick started, once again, to slip in, albeit more easily this time.

"'Now, you're talking, baby,' she whimpered. 'Now, you are *finally* starting to get the idea.'

"I pushed in a couple inches. Her ass was the tightest thing I had ever fucked. The only time I had ever even had a near-similar feeling was the time I cut a too-small hole in a cantaloupe I screwed in a hot summer field. The pleasure resulting from this submersion up cousin-butt was so enjoyable as to be actually painful.

"I kept shoving and shoving. She kept wiggling and wiggling her little ass, working it so that more of my inches slipped right inside.

"Apparently, though, I wasn't moving fast enough for her, any longer. Just the opposite— apparently, I now moved too goddamned slow.

"'Get *all* of your big dick on in there, you bastard!' she commanded. 'I want to really feel it. Push, push, fucking push!'

"So, I pushed harder. I arched my pelvis and brought it back down to ram a couple more inches of my dick up her ass. She groaned and wiggled her butt again.

"'More!' she squealed.

"So, I fed her more of my stiff meat. She was so tight that every inch of me into her was like ramming through a knothole two sizes too small. The shaft of my cock bowed under the exertion.

"Then, suddenly, her rear passage just seemed to open wide and let me slide the rest of the way, like a train gliding nonstop through a tunnel. My lower belly suddenly whacked her upturned ass, and my balls banged against her upturned backside.

"I don't know how she could have ever taken all of me. I mean, I am *really* big. Some girls have complained when I jabbed all of my peter up their snatches. But this time, I actually had all of me up a hole that didn't have its owner complaining. Eve took each and every inch of me. What's more, she loved each and every inch she had, too.

"'Fuck me, baby! And fuck me good! I fucking love it!'

"Unfortunately, I wasn't quite used to anything quite as tight as her ass. The pleasure was almost too much even before I started actually to pump. I just gritted my teeth and tried to prevent my climax from coming. But there was no way I could have stemmed those tides, so I didn't.

"My nuts let loose their creamy load with frantic cannon-shots that shook me from my head to my toes.

"After which, I realized Eve was laughing.

"'You are just a baby boy,' she said. 'You can't even hold off like a man.'

"Jesus, when she said that, I swore to God that my cock wasn't about to go soft just because I'd already blasted one load. I knew, too, that there was more than a good chance of my making good on that promise. There had been times when I had masturbated three times in a row before my old pecker finally started losing its starch.

"Well, when my dick stayed hard, and I started humping her asshole for sloppy seconds, that broad had a different tune to sing. It wasn't more than three seconds before she was back to grunting like the stuck pig she was and enjoying every damned minute of it.

"She babbled like crazy, moaned, and uttered all sorts of gibberish that I couldn't understand. After I had fucked her steadily for a solid five minutes, I noticed that her eyes had gone all glassy, and her mouth was drooling spit.

"I had reached a point where I didn't give a damn whether I ripped her wide open. This broad had my cock up her ass and, more importantly, was going to know it was there, doing what it was doing. I could always tell my parents that Eve had gotten me so hot and bothered that I couldn't help myself. After that talk I'd had with the old man, just a few days previously, I figured my parents would be quick enough to believe the very worst I could say about Eve.

"I watched my cousin's face for a long time and then centered my attention on her boobs. Those two jelly-like masses were just shaking like sixty on her ribcage. They were really something to see, let me tell you. I mean, they were really sweet-Jesus whoppers.

"Then, I looked farther—all of the way to her snatch. And since I was pretty limber from gymnastics at school, I decided to try something on Eve that I hadn't tried on any other girl. I decided this was my opportunity to see how good I was at eating out pussy. So, still with my big cock up her tight asshole, I just bent my head down and affixed my mouth to the pouty lips of her snatch.

"I'd heard a lot of guy-talk about eating pussy. I'd heard how it was *really* what the dames liked. One guy told me that once you'd tongued a bitch she was yours for life.

"So, while my cock fucked Eve's bunghole, my tongue fucked her twat. And, Jesus, did that girl ever go bongos! She started making all sorts of loud noises that were even more animalistic than the ones she'd been making before.

"I just buried my old tongue so deeply down her cunt that I thought I might actually touch China. Then, her hands were clawing away in my hair. At first, I thought she was trying to pull my head away. But she was actually trying to shove my face down even closer.

"And, yes, just like I heard it would be, her pussy smelled like fish, and it had a decidedly oily taste to it. None of which really did all that much *for me*, but it was really turning *her* on. And I wanted her to get turned on a whole lot. I wanted her to realize that this skinny, pimply-faced kid could give her the kind of butt fuck and cunt-gobble that she'd never had before and would be hard-pressed to get again.

"In about ten minutes, because of the extreme tightness of her asshole, I was on the verge of yet another nuts-rumble. I went back to trying to hold off my inevitable explosion. My cock and its cockhead just kept ballooning, bigger and bigger, inside her with each and every stroke I gave.

"I pulled my face away from her cunt, tired of the taste and the smell.

"'No, please, keep eating,' she protested and moaned.

"But I didn't give a shit whether *she* wanted more of anything. In fact, I figured to leave her wanting more. I figured to have her wanting me back for *mucho* repeats, once this particular session was over.

"I really started to concentrate on royally pumping her ass. My cock's juice puddled inside her and made her anal pit as lubricated as it could be.

"I slipped my hands under her ass to heave her even farther up and over my erection.

"Then, the tempo of my fucking went into genuinely high gear. No doubt, I was fast approaching *my* point of no return. I just turned into a human piston. I started puffing, panting, and gasping for breath. My body turned sweaty and wet with perspiration.

"Eve screamed and shouted, off into yet another climax. If I'd counted right, give or take a couple, that bitch climaxed about five times after my dick slid up her tight asshole.

"While my cock continued working, Eve started finger-fucking her snatch. Every time I'd heave my prick up her rectum, she'd jab her hand deep up her pussy. A few times, my cock actually felt her fingers working away inside her vagina. That was really wild. It was like she was masturbating me with her hand at the same time I was fucking her bunghole; hell, maybe that *was* what was happening.

"Our fucking bodies made all kinds of wet sounds.

"We were one machine out to achieve one purpose: mutual orgasm.

"I couldn't hold back. I had this tremendous desire to really blast up her butt. I bucked on top of her a few more times and, then, splattered her climax-spasming anal cavity with another steamy load of my hot spunk.

"I just kept letting go, and letting go, and letting to, until I had reached my last. I must have pumped enough slime up her ass to float the Queen Mary. I could tell by the expression on her face that she'd really enjoyed it, too. Suddenly, she just had this kind of dreamy expression, if you know what I mean.

"She finally opened her eyes, which had been closed during her final climax. She looked at me and smiled widely. She licked her lips so that I could see her pink tongue.

"'You may look like shit, but you *do* put out one hell of a nice butt-fuck,' she told me. And that was all I was waiting to hear. Then, she said: 'You get it hard again, honey, and I'll let you hump my ass again.'

"'Hell,' I said, suddenly very satisfied with myself. 'I could get a better piece of ass than you by fucking any neighborhood dog.'

"With that, I pulled out my softening prick, picked up my pants and my shirt from the floor, and left her and the room.

"That could have been the worst *cutting-off-of-my-nose- to-spite my-face* thing to do. After all, she was a very convenient for fucking and a good butt-fuck to boot.

"As it turned out, though, I'd played my cards just right. That very same night, she came begging me to put my big dick once again to work stirring the shit up her funky female asshole."

* * * * * * *

THIS CASE IS REALLY a study of hostility as evidenced by both Adam and Eve, directed mainly at their respective parents. The cousins' acts of mutual intercourse were merely the means by which they worked out their hostilities; the fact that incest was a factor was merely icing on the proverbial cake.

Eve's rebellion was the more aggressive. While Adam did, in fact, attempt to initiate the action, it was Eve who seemed to be more in control.

An examination of the girl's background throws more light on the probable cause.

Eve's mother, Marge, had always been a *wild* one, even before her marriage to Eve's father, Paul. Marge had, in fact, originally met Paul in a notorious singles' bar well-known for its promiscuous women. When the two took up a rather heated and—according to Eve who got the story from relatives—*disgraceful* romance, their affair was hardly looked upon favorably by the rest of Paul's family. The marriage of the two, conducted by a Justice of the Peace, was boycotted by Paul's relatives who refused, outright, to be in any way associated with *such a woman.*

Marge's pregnancy with Eve only held her down for a short time. She was partying it up to the moment she went into labor and was, in fact, taken from a bar to the hospital delivery room.

From the beginning, Eve was unwanted.

The following is a segment of recorded conversation taken in a short interview with Marge:

> If it hadn't have taken so much fucking time out of my social life, I would have had an abortion.

State Thorpe and Katz in their *The Psychology of Abnormal Behavior*:

> Much of the individual's inner hostility results from the basic anxiety he experiences. The child becomes resentful and hostile toward individuals (parents or parent-figures) who cause him to feel helpless, isolated and unwanted.

Eve began to act out her hostility as soon as she was old enough to do so. As we have seen, the rebellion eventually took a sexual direction. That Eve was physically mature for her age, having menstruated as early as age six, was probably one of the main factors that decided her upon sex rather than another outlet. She most likely indulged in flamboyant sex as much for attention as for rebellion. While Eve's mother was really too busy to pay much attention to her daughter's exploits, the rest of the community wasn't.

Eve had been called into the principal's office at school more than once for having been caught letting boys feel her up. And that she was famous, or rather infamous, in her neighborhood can be attested to by her own words:

> Every time I walked by a house, you could see mothers yanking their sweet little lambs inside. They thought for sure I was going to rape their little boys, right there on the spot. The truth of the matter is that I *did* manage to get my share of those boys' virgin cocks, no matter how much their mothers tried to keep them from me. For instance, take little Bobby Wilkins. He was the one who got me pregnant. I'm sure his mother didn't even think he knew what nooky was. Damned, she must have been one hell of a shocked bitch when she first found out that her little baby had begun the process of making a baby of his very own.

Again, it was Thorpe and Katz who said:

...hostility can...be expressed by embittered individuals in a pattern of nonconformity to socially accepted codes of behavior. These hostile individuals often evidence a serious lack of ethical and moral awareness. This lack of social, ethical, and moral awareness is referred to as a character disorder, a form of neurotic disturbance.

And Karen Horney, in *The Neurotic Personality of Our Time*, sheds a bit more light on the subject of Eve's rebellion:

A child can stand a great deal of what is often regarded as traumatic—such as sudden weaning, occasional beating, sex experiences—so long as inwardly he feels wanted and loved. Needless to say, a child feels keenly whether love is genuine....

Adam's rebellion differed from Eve's in the form it took. While the fact remains that his plans to initiate his affair with his cousin would indicate the emergence of an aggressive rebellion, his had been more of a repressed rebellion up to that time. As a matter of fact, an interview with his parents, I am sure, would have revealed their total ignorance of the forces at work within Adam at the time of his incestuous relationship with Eve.

Adam, unlike Eve, was known to the neighborhood and school as a friendly, polite, easy-going boy. To have told anyone that he had actually had intercourse, not only once but several times, with his first cousin would have brought gasps of disbelief. However, the fact does remain that he did do just that.

Say Thorpe and Katz:

> Strong parental and social pressures cause the child to fear to express his anger and resentment. As a result many children repress their feelings of hostility. Outwardly they may appear affable, complaisant, and cooperative. They are 'nice' children and good citizens. But underneath their affability lies an undercurrent of anger and rage. They have learned they dare not show their true hostile feelings.

Adam's rebellion centered about the strictness of his parents, and the fact that he resented their treating him as a child when he had long since reached puberty. At age sixteen, he had been caught masturbating by his mother and was "whipped like a little baby" for doing such a "foul and filthy thing."

Contributing to his growing resentment of his parents was the fact that they were constantly reprimanding him and joking about his awkwardness and acne. Adam was often made the butt of cutting remarks by both his mother and father.

It was Robert W. White, in his *The Abnormal Personality*, who pointed out:

> The body, including both its competence and its attractiveness, takes a

significant place in the development of self-esteem, especially between the ages of 5 and 20. Any marked deviations from the norm, unless they are on the side of athletic ability in boys and beauty in girls, are likely to create sharp feelings of inferiority....

It was also White who went on to say:

In a relatively integrated personality which, enjoys reasonable esteem somewhere, feelings of inferiority will be absent or transient and of small importance.

Adam sought to find his "reasonable esteem" elsewhere by capitalizing on his overly developed genitals. Quite large by normal standards, Adam's penis, testicles (and scrotum) became his passport to success with the opposite sex. At ages of sexual exploration, many of Adam's dates consented to go out with him *only* to touch, see, and/or have sexual intercourse with someone of Adam's fabled genitalia size.

As for the anal orientation of Adam and Eve's incestuous affair, it is difficult to decide whether Eve was actually "numbed" by so much vaginal intercourse to desire something new and exciting, or whether she was merely searching for one more means of acting out her rebellion against parental norms.

While constant intercourse, as witnessed by statements of professional prostitutes, does often tend to lessen the degree of enjoyment to be had from normal coitus, I would tend to believe—due to Eve's extreme youth—that in Eve's case her desire for anal penetration was purely another flaunting of societal rules and regulations.

Say Thorpe and Katz:

> Probably the most severe and damaging expression of hostility is when the individual acts it out in an antisocial fashion. This is the condition of aggressive rebellion. It includes a variety of negative, defiant, non-conforming, and destructive actions.... The antisocial...type acts out his hostile feelings in order to hurt or injure other human beings....

* * * * * * *

"AFTER THAT DAY, Eve and I really ended up fucking up a storm. The only real problem, as far as I was concerned, was that she never really ever let me ram it up her pussy for more than a couple times. She really didn't like prick up her snatch half as much as she enjoyed it working up her tight behind.

"Anyway, her ass was snugger than her cunt, so it was no big problem for me, in the end (pun intended, by the way). I decided that it didn't much matter to me *where* I blasted my nuts, just as long as I got to blast them somewhere inside her. And she was a lot better, a lot more experienced a screw, than most of those *come-get-our-cunts* babes back in that school I went to.

"It really got exciting when Eve started coming to my room during the night on a regular basis. The idea of having my dear parents sleeping just down the hall, while I was banging my cousin's butt, really made our humps seem extra exciting. At any time, my mother or father might well have heard our noises and come to check on the cause.

"We had to be quiet, had to try to control our grunting and our groaning. The walls of the house were thick but not *that* thick. You could hear things happening pretty far away. But the fact that we had to bite our lips and tongues, plug our mouths with sheet, only added to our excitement.

"My parents continued to eye us for signs that something *was* going on between us. I remember that Wednesday I lied about the headache and came home from school early to bung-fuck Eve, my old man got home early, too, and realized I was there when I shouldn't have been; I think he saw my school books lying in one of the downstairs chairs. He hit those stairs like a race horse. I could hear him taking them three steps at a time. Anyway, it wasn't more than a couple of seconds before he was standing in my bedroom. I think he actually expected to come up and find Eve and me rutting on my bed, but Eve and I had finished ages before. My parents really thought Eve was a temptress just waiting for the moment she could take away their dear little son's cherry.

"The poor old parents didn't know that I hadn't been a virgin since about age eight. That was when a couple of us guys went off and fucked around with each other down by the river. Of course, there hadn't been any cum, then, but there sure a hell had been of a lot of *feel-real-goods*.

"But back to my old man's running up the stairs to catch Eve and me screwing. He really looked shocked as hell when I was the only one on the bed. By that time, I was even dressed again.

"He asked me what was wrong, why I was home from school ahead of time. I told him just what I'd told the nurse. I had this splitting headache. He believed me. A headache was a good excuse. I had sinus problems and used to get sinus headaches all of the time. We even went to a doctor about it, once, and he prescribed some pills for me to take. I had even made it a point to take one of those pills out of its bottle that I had on hand. Knowing my suspicious mother, I figured she'd probably go count them if I told her I'd taken one.

"That evening, I came down to supper and told everyone I was feeling a lot better. I sat down at the table, and there was Eve. She really didn't have too much to say. She didn't smile or even look at me. She just ate her food like the prim and proper lady my parents would have *liked* her to be.

"I'm sure my parents were surprised at how good Eve came across. I know damned good and well they had expected her to be a bitch to take care of. But Eve played it really cool. She acted like the perfect little lady when around them. Of course, they never dreamed that she was creeping into my room, behind their backs, and acting like a whore with me each and every night.

"After Eve and I started screwing around regularly, my mother did comment that I was beginning to look just 'a wee haggard.' I told her it was all the tests they were giving me at school. She took it in stride, and the old man commented that it was all part of 'the educational process.' Little did he know. But then I guess sex *is* a vital part of education, isn't it?

"But let me go back to that first night little Eve turned up in my room after all the lights had gone out. You know, it was funny, but I was expecting her to come. I had even gone so far as to leave my door partly open just for her. Nor was I wearing pajamas.

"I didn't usually sleep stark naked, before Eve; if the old lady had ever learned I'd opted for wearing nothing, she would have shit bricks. She told me, more than once, that a gentleman 'never sleeps without his PJ's.' Well, that night, I took off those PJ's and shoved them way under my bed. I lay there, underneath just one sheet, and I started to play with myself. As a matter of fact, I had already blasted my rocks once before Eve showed up. I'd gotten a bit carried away with my thoughts of ramming my thick tool, once again, up her tight little asshole and had ended up spurting my gooey cream all over my chest and belly and chin. I was wiping up the mess when she made her appearance.

"She came over to the bed and didn't say a thing. She was only wearing a robe, and she let it drop quickly. I saw her luscious jugs suspended in front of her in seeming defiance of gravity.

"She pulled back the sheet to uncover me. She laid down right on top of me, and I felt her hairy cunty nuzzling my masturbation-limped prick.

"'What's wrong, Studly, can't you get it up?'

"I felt like telling her that *it* had already been up, now down, and I'd cum without her (didn't she smell the cum-soaked Kleenexes tossed beneath my bed with my PJ's?). Instead, I told her that my dick would get hard enough fast enough if she'd suck on it a bit. I really didn't expect her to do it. But she did. She moved her face down over my crotch so damned fast that I hardly knew she was doing it until she was down there, my limp dick being gobbled up. She gave a couple healthy sucks and then spit it out. When she got swiftly up out of the bed, she wasn't smiling.

"'You goddamned little bastard!' she said. 'You've already creamed, I can taste and smell it.'

"She bopped back to her room, and that was the last time I saw her that particular evening. As a matter of fact, it was the last time I saw her for two evenings. I began to think that she wasn't going to come back at all.

"When Tuesday arrived, though, and she was still playing hard to get, I decided if she didn't come on over that night, I'd go to *her* room. Either that or I'd fake another headache the next day and come back to the house and fuck her.

"By Tuesday, this boy was hot as hell. I'd been too intent upon getting Eve again to fuck round elsewhere. I'd even slacked off on beating my meat in anticipation of screwing the real thing. I just knew nothing could give my pecker the kind of release it would get up her asshole. That one ass-fuck she had allowed me had started to seem to me to be the best piece of ass (literally) I'd ever had.

"God was I one happy dude when that very night she made her appearance. And this time, though sorely tempted, I hadn't jerked off before her arrival. My nuts were blue and bulged as big as baseballs.

"She dropped her robe, like the first time. She crawled into bed and rolled over on top of me. Only this time, my pecker was anything but soft. My cock, in fact, was painfully rock-hard.

"'Now, that's a far better hello than last time,' she said.

"She wiggled her hairy twat against me for the longest time. Then, she stopped and just rested against me.

"'Too bad you're such a goddamned novice,' she said finally. 'With equipment like yours, you've got great fuck potential. If you only had the know-how, you could have all the girls, including me, just eating out of your hand, while riding your big dick. You know what I'm talking about?'

"'What in the hell *are* you talking about? You want to fuck, or do you want to sit here and gab all goddamned night? If you want to gab, then go back to your room and talk to someone interested— yourself. It'll only take me a couple of seconds to beat off my dong so that I can get some sleep.'

"'I once was fucked by an older gentleman, about thirty,' she said. 'He was: a salesman out of St. Louis. Brother, that guy really knew how to please a girl. He knew a lot of things about pleasuring that I doubt you'll ever learn. Because I don't think you have the brains or the talent for it.'

"'What in the hell are you talking about, cunt?' I knew she was leading up to something.

"She rolled off of me and onto her belly on the bed. She reached her hands back to her ass and pulled open her buns. I thought that she was finally getting ready for me to plow my dick on in. I got up on my knees between her splayed legs and started to get my prick all wet with spit for the plunge.

"'You know what you'd do if you were a man instead of a mouse?' she challenged me. 'If you knew anything about sex at all, or how you could really please me, you'd stick your nose between the cheeks of my butt and lay a big wet kiss on my bung hole.'

"I thought she was joking. Eating out her snatch was one thing. Eating out her poop-shoot was quite another. Dining on ass was something we guys only talked about, usually with accompanying grimaces. I don't think I knew anyone, at least at the time, who had actually *done* it. Thinking she was pulling my leg, I hesitated a bit too long.

"'See there, you little baby,' she said. 'Go ahead then and just stick your big pecker up my ass, because that's all you're going to be adventuresome enough to do for the rest of your life. Dumb little dip-shits like you never do learn the real refinements of sex.'

"Well, once I realized that she *hadn't* been joking, actually *did* want my face pressed tightly against the butt hole, I didn't know what to do or say.

"'You want me to lick your ass? Is that what you're saying?' I had to be sure.

"'You got guts enough to do it, sonny boy? You got guts enough to show this woman that you're really a man who cares?'

"That was all it took. I didn't care whether she made the request to degrade me or not. Whatever, I went down to her butt and buried my nose right on in it.

"She used her hands to open her ass cheeks wider.

"I pulled back a bit (initially kind of repelled by the smell), moved my lips to her hole and, as originally requested, kissed it.

"'Now, fuck me with your tongue,' she whispered in command. 'Ram it deep, deep, deep up my asshole.'

"I licked her asshole pucker first. I remember thinking that it was rubbery and continued to smell decidedly of shit. Surprisingly enough, though, the thought of jabbing my tongue up inside it actually turned me on.

"I could also tell, by the way she was wiggling, that she was getting just as much pleasure out of my eating her ass as she'd insinuated she would get. And I ended up figuring that eating out butt couldn't be any grosser than eating out pussy. After all, she might shit out of this hole, but she pissed out of the other.

"I rolled my tongue into a tube and jabbed it into her anal love canal. Spit dribbled out of my mouth and ran the crease between her butt cheeks.

"'Tongue-fuck me, baby,' she said. 'And while you're at it, finger-fuck my twat.'

"Well, all of that was easy for her to say. She didn't have the one hell of a hard cock between *her* legs that I had between mine; my dick hadn't been beaten to climax for days. Even so, I was determined to play her little *prove-to-me-you're-a-real-man* game for a few minutes more.

"I stuck my hand beneath her and found her snatch. Her pussy had leaked a pool of sexual damp onto the sheet beneath her. I rammed my hand up her cunt, and it was like reaching into a washing-machine full of water-soaked clothes. I must have touched her clitoris, because that girl went absolutely nutters. She started squirming over my fingers like they were multiple-cocks going at her.

"At the same time, I pushed my tongue deeply up her butt and wiggled it there. I did that until she was squirming almost out of control. About that time, I finally decided that my cock had gone unsatisfied long enough, and I wasn't waiting any longer for an invitation to dick-fuck her asshole. I had gotten her anus so wet with spit that I figured my cock was going to have easy sailing all of the way inside.

"I heaved myself up into ass-fuck position, put my cock right where my tongue had just been, and I shoved on in.

"All this time, I had left my hand up her cunt, hoping that my fingers would keep her occupied so that she wouldn't make too big a deal about my substituting my cock for my tongue up her poop-shoot.

"But she must have been ready for my cock. About the same time I was sliding it up her, she heaved up on her hands and knees, dog-style, and back-thrust her ass to ram me full-depth on into her.

"'Doggy-fuck my butt, stud,' she said into a muffling pillow. 'Go ahead and Doberman-fuck me senseless.'

"I certainly didn't need a second invite. Once I realized that my cock was in her all of the way, the pleasure just flooded over me. The lust started building and continued non-stop.

"It was a comfortable position: she on her hands and knees, I kneeling behind her, my cock shoved into her rear.

"All this time, I continued working my hand up her leaking snatch. Her clitoris was so hard that I thought I played with a hard miniature prick. Her vagina was so goddamned wet that it was almost impossible to get my fingers to stay inside.

"I started hammering my prick home, marveling—for not the first time—at the unusually tight fit of her rectum, marveling at the excruciating joy of having my cock slide the lining of her bowel. I began drowning in a sea of wonderment that flowed from my swollen testicles into the rest of my body.

"I humped, humped, humped. I wanted to scream out my pleasure, cry out my warning that orgasm was near and that her ass was soon going to be filled to the brim with my love-juice. But I couldn't scream, because of my parents just down the hall. All I could do was increase my tempo. And the springs began to squeak dangerously loud with the force of our fucking. I thought my parents would probably hear us, for sure.

"My cock moved back and forth in her shit hole. I moved my hand back and forth in her snatch. She orgasmed at least four times beneath my dual attack on her body before I gave her anything but pre-seminal discharge. Every time her body climaxed, her asshole went spastic around my dick, and her vagina collapsed glove-like around my fingers.

"When *I* finally exploded, I really gave her quite a hefty load. I had sex cream inside my balls that had been there for days on end. I wanted her to have it all. So, I gave it all to her. I could feel all those thick seeming gallons letting loose, coursing up my steel-hard penis shaft, jettisoning out my quivering cock lips to baste her inner butt with all my delicious spunk. Her butt hole overflowed liquid, oozed it around my balls, dribbled it down the crease of her cock-fucked ass to slime the sheet between her legs.

"Once she groaned so loudly I thought for sure she'd been heard by the neighbors down the street.

"Even when I was finished with my exploding, collapsed out on top of her, my cock was still buried to its gnarly root. I was hoping that, maybe, I could somehow get up enough steam to fuck her again.

"She turned her head so she could see me.

"'You just might make a lover, yet, boy,' she said. 'Now, pull that thick cock of yours out of my ass and let me suck on it before I go back to my room.'

"I did just what she asked. I might have been older than she was, but as far as sex was concerned, I knew she was the boss. I figured I might as well let her do what she wanted. Besides, the very thought of her mouth wrapped about my cum-and-shit-slicked cock was, in itself, enough to make my dick start re-swelling. If anything was going to get me back into action fast, it would be her lips blowing my dick to complete stiffness. I had been sucked off by a few girls in my time—even by a few boys, for that matter—and I knew a good blow-job could be almost as good as a good fuck. Although, at that moment, I somehow doubted that anyone's sucking, even Eve's, could equal the pleasure I had when I cock-rammed her ass. No mouth or cunt could have been as tight as her butt was.

"I pulled out, rolled to my back, as instructed, flopped open my legs so that she could get to my *squirming-to-life-again* penis. And it wasn't two seconds before she was down there, her head buried over my meat, eating away, just as she'd promised.

"Her head started moving up and down, up and down, her mouth sucking away on my peter until my prick grew to be as hard as it had ever been. Her lips and tongue quickly wiped free all traces of the mess with which my cum and her shit had recently streaked it. Her tongue wrapped and rewrapped my sexual shaft, her nose burying in my pubic hair. Her chin pressed into my balls. She rode my groin like a horse rides a merry-go-round pole.

"Both her hands worked under my ass. As her mouth sucked on my hard-on, her fingertips petted *my* anal opening. She caressed my pucker and sucked my dick. Then, she started working her fingers *up* my asshole.

"I let her fingers poke and probe my butt hole. I'd had enough blow-jobs, had had enough fingers up my rectum, my own included, to know that prostate stimulation complemented any suck-off really nicely. I liked prostate-petting fingers yanked out of my ass just as I was climaxing. I wondered if I should tell her that but, in the end (pun intended) figured, that if anyone knew what I wanted, when I wanted it, it would be Eve.

"When my nuts finally erupted, Eve did know exactly what to do, too. She played with my walnut prostate for the first part of my orgasm and, only then, removed her fingers from my butt in a way that doubled my pleasure and fun.

"I really gave her a mouthful of spunk, by way of reward. And she took it all, not spilling a dewy drop. She swallowed it down, her throat muscles milking my meat like a baby greedily sucking its mother's teat.

"'You have one really smelly asshole,' she *pot-calling-the-kettle-black* said when she was done, licking her lips. 'I could smell it the whole damned time I was eating your dick.' With that, she got up, put on her robe and left the room.

"For the whole two-and-one-half remaining weeks that Eve stayed with us, I really don't think my parents ever once suspected that the two of us were actually getting it on, sexually.

"We were only once *almost* caught. That was on one of those days Eve went to the hospital to see her mother. She always made it a point to come back to the house early so the two of us could grab a quick fuck in the basement, even if one or both of my parents were home at the time.

"Our basement was a shambles. My father was in the process of having it remodeled; it was kind of like a hobby for him. He had been working on it, at it, on and off, for about a year, and you couldn't see much improvement. He only got to work on it on weekends, and most of those weekends had someone always persuading him to go play golf instead. So, amid the mess and the clutter of sawdust, timber, and all sorts of weird-looking tools, and dangling wires and insulation, Eve and I fucked on a blanket.

"Mom hardly ever came down into the basement, because she'd once tripped on one of dad's carelessly placed power tools and had almost broken a leg.

"That particular day, I waited for Eve, upstairs, by the basement door and by the adjoining outside backdoor. It was very simple for her to get into the house from the backyard, without being seen by my mother who, like on that day, *was* at home. Eve only had to sneak up, behind the concealment of our neighbor's hedge, and I would quietly, when the coast was clear, let her in.

"We got her safely into the house and into the basement. Soon we were both stripped down, naked as jays and on the blanket. I knew that, before we were through, I would end up fucking her ass but, until that happened, I just wasn't able to resist another chance to eat out her luscious pussy for which, by then, I'd acquired a real appetite.

"I went to my knees between her open legs, working both of my hands underneath her naked ass cheeks. I lifted her hips a little so that I could more easily get to her sweet cunty.

"She was hot, too, because the lips of her snatch were automatically gaped to give me a good view of the raw-looking variegated pink flesh inside it. Her clitoris was swollen and eagerly offering itself for some gentle licking.

"She knew what I was doing, and I knew that she wanted me to do it; I didn't have to look at her face to know that, either.

"She reached her hands down and pulled her gaping snatch even wider for my viewing pleasure. She wiggled her hips and gave me a first-hand look at just what was in store for my tongue and for me.

"She spread her legs as wide as possible. I dragged my tongue down one of her thighs. I moved my face back up again and found the base of her vagina slit and ran my tongue along the lips of it. As I did so, her twat leaked a mess of oily juice that was wet and tasty on my tongue.

"I moved my mouth in closer, clamping my lips shut around her swollen clit. The minute I did, she threw her legs up and over my shoulders. In this position, I had ideal access to all the wonders her pussy had to offer.

"She was really turned on. Her face was all twisted up. Her eyes were glassy. She was licking her lips.

"There was a smell between her legs that was heady and not at all unpleasant.

"I gripped her bare ass for support, and then I came down hard on her sex with my face. My tongue slipped and slid along her swollen cunt lips. I teased her clit. I moved my tongue back and forth over every possible inch of her raw, wet, and wonderful vagina.

"I really gave her hole a working over.

"She started writhing like a mad woman. Her moans got louder. Her cunt overflowed so much lubricating fluid that I was hard-pressed to lick it all up.

"When I felt her body start to stiffen for orgasm, I jabbed a couple of my fingers up her butt. I worked those fingers up her rectum like sixty, even as I tongue-fucked her twat.

"I stuck my tongue so far inside of her that I thought for sure I was licking her tonsils from the bottom-up. I pulled my tongue back to lap, yet again, at her clit, battling with it as if my tongue were a boxer, her clitoris a punching bag.

"Her head dropped back, almost as if her neck were broken. She sobbed with pleasure. Baby, that bitch was on the edge.

"Just about then, the basement door opened. I heard Mom say something.

"There were sounds of descending footsteps.

"A neighbor had come over to borrow one of dad's saws. Seemingly, my old man had told him to come over *any time* and pick it up. *Any time* was inconveniently, for us, then and there.

"Eve was so far along toward orgasm that there was no goddamned way that she could stop it. She'd tell me later that, at the time, she hadn't even known we'd been joined.

"I pulled my mouth from her erupting snatch and prayed she wasn't making as much noise as I was sure she *was* making.

"I fell in even closer to her and clamped my hand over her mouth. If I could no longer hear her, I could feel and see her still climaxing beneath me.

"Luckily for us, the guy found the saw he was looking for on a sawhorse at the very bottom of the stairs. It only took him a quick second to get it and retreat back up the stairs to my waiting mother.

"But, you know, the very fact that we had almost been discovered only added to our pleasure, not only that time in the basement but all of the other times, in the basement, or elsewhere.

"The appearance and disappearance of the neighbor left my cock so rigid and hard that Eve, as soon as she spotted it, rolled over on her belly and spread her asshole for my enormous stiff meat to have-at-it.

"I jumped right on, the tip of my cock oozing juice like an artesian well oozing water.

"I put my hands to her ass cheeks, worked a couple of my fingers into her asshole. I felt her tight anal muscles initially protest but, then, relax after a few seconds of massage. I pulled my fingers free and aimed the tip of my slime-covered cock to the same entranceway of her sweet behind. As I did so, my dick provided another gush of natural lubricant that pooled atop and within the fine hair that grew the cleavage formed by the curves of her butt cheeks.

"I placed the head of my dick to and through her sphincter. Her anal muscles were relaxed enough from my finger-fuck to take my dick easily, from its top to its bottom.

"My belly soon pressed tightly against her buns.

"I pulled back, dragging the shaft of my prick until only its massive head was once again gummed by her butt lips. I lowered into her so quickly, this next time, that my swinging balls whacked her ass and sent pleasurable pain into the pit of my again-butt-smashing belly.

"I opened my legs, letting them fall to either side of hers. Then I brought my legs toward each other again so that I was holding her closed legs tightly between mine. This made her ass grip my prick like a pair of pliers. I started pumping.

"She muttered something into the blanket.

"My cock up her butt was really getting to her, already. I really gave her a few hard pumps, jiggling my hips so that my cock stirred in her, like a spoon in a bowl. I pushed a hand beneath her so that I was finger-fucking her cunt, at one and the same time I cock-fucked her asshole. I jabbed my hand up her snatch so damned far that I could feel my own cock working her from the other side.

"I started licking her ear and throat, tonguing her skin. There was an artery in her neck that throbbed against my sensitive lips.

"Again, I pulled my prick almost entirely free of her spasming a-hole. Again, I jabbed back in. I could feel her ass walls expand to take my inches: stretch as my penis moved in, collapse as my prick moved outward. My tube-like sausage really explored her hole.

"She had one tight anus to explore, too, let me tell you. It could really chow down on my cock when it wanted. It was a toothless anal mouth seemingly designed just for my gumming-me pleasure.

"'Hard!' she demanded. 'Fuck me fucking hard!'

"She kept saying it over and over and over. Each time my prick jammed up her hole, she said it. Each time my prick pulled out, she said it. Within my pauses, she said it.

"Our bodies were soon sweating like Swedes in a sauna.

"I kept raising and lowering my dick, ramming it back and forth through the tightness of her body. And inside her, my cock must have really been leaking, because her asshole was really wet and slick and fucking-a wonderful.

"My nuts started elevating. They bulged larger with all the cream they were soon going to be asked to ejaculate. My thigh muscles tighten. My chest, stomach, and arms went all weak and funny.

"All of this time, my hand kept pumping her cunt. She moved her body sensuously beneath me, and over my fingers, as my prick kept going at her via her backdoor.

"My prick swelled larger and larger up her anal sheathe. My nuts got bigger and bigger until they ached with desire to get rid of their loads.

"While I fucked, I pictured the expression that would register on my mom's face if she was to come down those steps, again, and see her little baby-boy's man-penis buried up Eve's woman-asshole, my fingers buried up Eve's twat. Thinking of that made my pleasure all the greater.

"Jesus, did I blast when I blasted! Every fiber of my being tensed with the discharge. Muscles in my legs bunched with the pleasure. I went stiff as a board all over. My balls grouped tightly to the base of my prick. I couldn't help but moan the intensity of my increasing ecstasy.

"At the same time, Eve orgasmed beneath me. Her ass squeezed my dick. I thought that her butt was going to press my exploding meat to nothingness. Her vagina spasmed about my hand, fluttered so that I thought my fingers were being beaten to death by birds' wings.

"That fuck was really, *really* great. My hips, even as I climaxed, were like a jack-hammer out of control. I just banged her, fucked her, and screwed her silly.

"The two of us did our sexual dance, there on the blanket, there on the floor, there in that basement, my mother (and the neighbor?) somewhere (still?) above us.

"When we were done, finally, we were pooped. We just lie there and said nothing.

"Those basement screws with Eve were so intense, even thinking about them, today, takes my breath away.

"Of course, this screwing around with my cousin only lasted the short time she was with us. Her mother—damn it!—finally got out of the hospital.

"When Eve went home with her mom that was really the last I ever saw of her—at least sexually.

"I really hated to see her go, too, as you can well imagine. She had me addicted to screwing asshole, especially *her* asshole. To this day, whenever I get the choice between screwing twat *or* butt, I always take the butt. Not that cunt turns me off. But ass, since Eve, can really get me going. I don't think, though, that I've found a butt since Eve's that's quite as tight or as good. But then that only gives me the incentive to keep on looking, doesn't it?"

ANAL COUSINS, BY WILLIAM MALTESE

III.

WHAT THE DOCTOR ORDERED

"**I WORKED IN A DEPARTMENT** store that stayed open late on Mondays and Fridays. This one Monday; several of us girls had to stay even later, after closing, when one of the cash registers came up short. When we finally figured out where the money had gone and could leave, it was *really* late, actually early morning. It was dark, and the streets were completely empty.

"One of the girls offered to give me a lift to my apartment, but I said no. She looked at me as if I was crazy to even think of walking the city streets at that hour, but I only smiled. Some of the girls thought they were going to be attacked at any and all times of the day or night, but I wasn't one of them—then. I'd walked home a lot of the time when it was dark, and nothing had ever happened. As a matter of fact, walking home was kind of thrilling. At least in those days. I actually used to fantasize rapists, hiding and ready to jump out, as I walked by.

"I left the store, walked for a couple of blocks, turned a corner and walked for a couple more blocks. My apartment house wasn't that far. As a matter of fact, from the tenth floor of the department store in which I worked, I could see the roof of my building.

"I'd gotten about halfway there when I started thinking that there *was* someone following me. Whenever I stopped, the footsteps seemingly behind me would stop, too. But you know how people let their imaginations run away with them? Well, I was determined not to let mine run away with me. When the sounds that seemed to be following me suddenly up and stopped, I felt blessedly relieved and berated myself for having been so foolish as to have imagined them, there, in the first place.

"*They* came out of nowhere and pulled me into the alley. It was all so sudden, I didn't know what in the hell was happening. I didn't even have a chance to scream. There was an agonizing hurt on the left side of my head where someone hit me. I staggered into the darkness. I remember colliding hard against a brick wall.

"I must have been knocked completely out, because suddenly there was nothing: nothing but the pain that is; the pain stayed with me even when I was unconscious.

"When the mist finally began to clear, I had a big thick Negro cock jammed up my snatch. It was so big that its bulk was threatening to rip my hole.

"I couldn't see the face of the man on top of me distinctly. But he *was* black. That much I could tell. His heavy breath and his body stunk like a pig that hadn't washed in years. He made these animalistic, little piggy grunts and groans.

100

"My body was filled with his dick and the pain it was causing. I couldn't really believe, even then, what was happening to me. I was just numb. I laid there drowning in the pain, not really comprehending what any of it was all about.

"When I finally did realize I was being raped, and raped royally, I tried to struggle, tried to push him off. I tried to scream, but someone, or something, again hit me against the side of the head. It was useless for me to battle, utterly useless. So, I just lay there, hoping that the horror would soon be over and done.

"My legs were spread-eagled, his cock humping my snatch, in between, like crazy. I remember trying to sob, remember tasting blood. I started to whimper.

"'Shut your goddamned mouth, bitch, or I'll shut it for you, once and for all,' someone said. And it wasn't the guy who was fucking me. There were others, in the darkness, standing around—*Oh, dear God, help me!*—watching.

"The one on top of me started fucking all the harder, really started moving all of his black meat back and forth, up and down, round and round, in my sore snatch. I was really in pain, and it wasn't because I was virgin. I'd had plenty of cock up me, before. But this black man must have really had a whopper. His fullness stretched my poor vagina to capacity. My twat couldn't have expanded any farther if it had wanted to—and it *did* want to. Every time he lowered into me, it was like someone had taken an ever-expanding red-hot spike and jammed it up my guts.

"Any groan that I did uncontrollably manage only seemed to excite, all the more, the black man on top of me. He gave me some more of his powerful strokes, jamming my hole full of his pecker, and then pulling up his hips so most of his dick pulled out. His peter was so long that I thought he would never withdraw to the end of it, and then never stop feeding it back in. I thought for sure, on his every inward drive, that he was going to poke on through my belly and stuff the head of his prick into the base of my throat.

"His balls banged the crease of my ass. He grunted exertions. His face was sweaty.

"I gritted my teeth. There were tears in my eyes. My body felt more and more pain. I prayed that I could pass out, again, and remain in unknowing darkness while all of it happened and was finished.

"He just kept battering away at my guts, though: thrusting, pulling out, thrusting, pulling out, and thrusting. His heavy cock was bruising each and inch of my cunt.

"Then, suddenly, there was the feel of his jism white-washing my whole insides. His black body went into grand-mal seizure atop me. He must have had a gallon of the spunk stored in his big black balls, because it just kept coming and coming, and coming. I didn't have room for all of it *and* his dick. I was ballooned to near explosion by the both of them.

"I passed out, again.

"Too soon, I regained consciousness, my pain not over. There was another, albeit smaller-dicked, black man on top of me, pumping away just as heartily as the guy there before him.

"My cunt was on fire. My guts were raw. My throat was full of my puke. My chest ached. Every inch of me, body and soul, ached.

"The second man's prick just kept clawing away at my guts. It kept ramming into those raw regions of my snatch already worked over and damaged.

"Something warm trickled down my leg; it wasn't natural lubricating sex juice, his or mine; nor was it his cum. It was my blood; I was ripped and bleeding.

"Whether I was in pain or bleeding to death, though, didn't make a hell of a lot of difference to my rapists. The second Negro just kept plugging away. His large balls kept flopping hard, fast, furious, and sweat-wet against my bruised ass.

"I reached a point, finally, where I was hardly aware of his meat inside me. My pain blessedly numbed me.

"I still wanted to cry out, but I still couldn't get anything to come out of my agony-constricted throat.

"I squeezed my eyes shut and continued to hope, in vain, that it would all go away, or I'd wake up and find it was just a horrible nightmare.

"I projectile-vomited.

"'Jesus, the fucking bitch has puked again!' my rider exclaimed. But his saying so didn't keep him from pumping away.

"A few seconds later, there was another deluge of spermal black-man's gunk blasted up my hole.

"I don't remember exactly, to this day, how many of those black men climbed on and off me in that alley on that night. I do know that there were at least five of them. And all of them were hung like horses, some more so than others. I remember being screwed by the first and the second. Then, it all gets rather vague, but I think I was fucked by two more. *Then,* there was the one I really don't think I'll ever forget to my dying day.

"The very fraction of a second his big pecker rammed halfway into me, and he tried so desperately to get in the rest of his dick, I finally found the long and loud scream I'd been looking for to express all of the monstrous horror I was feeling and had been forced to feel. Even I was surprised to hear me, since I was, by then, pretty much convinced that I'd been struck dumb.

"'Jesus, can someone shut her up!' someone said loudly.

"I screamed again. Someone hit me again. I didn't care. I screamed again.

"A police squad car found me in the alley.

"Am ambulance took me to the hospital.

"I was in pretty bad shape. I lost a lot of blood. I was only semi-conscious for nearly five days. Occasionally, the mist would clear, and I'd see forms or faces. I remember my father and my mother. I also remember wondering just what *they* were doing there. We didn't even live in the same city.

"Every so often, my pain would start up again, coming back to me through the fog, and I'd start to moan and groan. And someone in white would always come to me. And in another minute or two, I'd sink back into blessed nothingness.

"After I got to regaining full consciousness more regularly, actually, definitely, recognizing people, my gang-rape was the last thing I wanted to remember or talk about.

"Nonetheless, I eventually did go down to police headquarters to look at mug shots and at a couple of lineups. But all black men, on paper, and in real life, looked the same to me. I couldn't very well ask the policemen to pull down every black man's pants so I could check out the size and shape of his dick. Anyway, I didn't ask, even if I could have. All Negro pricks are so goddamned big, anyway, aren't they? I doubt even pulling down my potential assailants' pants would have done me much good in recognizing them.

"More than once, I told the police as much about the incident as I could remember—which wasn't much. But I didn't talk about it with my parents or with friends. Everyone, but the police, conveniently was content to let me avoid the subject. People acted rather like I had been put in the hospital because I had pneumonia, stomach flu, or something like that. They asked after my health, sent flowers and cute get-well cards.

"When I was sent home, my parents checked into a nearby hotel. They thought they should be close. They were kind, sweet, and concerned. But what could they really *say* to their daughter who had been gang-raped? Just what really could they *do* for their daughter who had been gang-raped? Actually, there wasn't really too much that anyone could say or do. Mom and dad spent most of their time walking around and looking very sad-eyed and very embarrassed. And I, after only a short while, was made uneasy by their being there.

"I told them that I was feeling much better and that they should go home. They looked appropriately distraught and protested, but they knew and I knew, that they were anxious to leave me and return to their less traumatic existence in middle-America.

"I went back to my job at the department store. And after awhile, the whole horrid incident just seemed to be a very-bad dream. I almost succeeded in shoving the whole thing completely away into its own little hidden nook in the very back of my mind.

"Then, for two months in a row, I didn't menstruate. I panicked. I went to a doctor who told me I was pregnant. I went into hysterics, right then and there, in his office. He had to call two nurses to hold me down while he administered a sedative and called to check me into the psychiatric wing of the hospital.

"I went through all the red-tape to get an abortion, accompanied by the loud clamor of reporters and right-to-lifers, the latter with their disgusting and disturbing pickets that showed aborted fetuses.

"I lived my gang-rape all over again, made worse by my knowing that there was suddenly some *thing* growing inside of me that was the direct result of one violently monstrous black cock, among many, that had been uninvited in its painful thrusts to climax inside me. There was an abomination sprouting, more heinous than cancer, in my womb, that was going to have to be cut out of me.

"There would be more blood! There would be more pain!

"Again, my mother and father came to the city to stay. They really didn't know, for sure, what to say, this time. They really didn't know what to do, this time. There was really nothing for them to say or do, except provide appropriately sad faces and expressions of sympathy and moral support. None of which helped me; although I'm sure it helped them.

"I had been gang-raped. I was pregnant. I was going to have an abortion. It all sounds so simple, so clear cut. But I don't think anyone will ever really know the sheer agony I went through, the torment, the utter emotional strain.

"I was in such a state that the doctors actually didn't know whether or not I would be able to take the stress of the abortion. They told me that they thought that, maybe, we should postpone *everything* until I got my strength (mental and physical) back. I went into another fit of hysteria. I felt if they waited too long, it would suddenly become impossible to abort the abomination. I didn't want the monster. I didn't want it to live a fraction of a second longer than circumstances demanded. I wanted it sliced out of me, the sooner the better.

"They gave me the abortion. I bled. They thought I was going to die. They put me in the Emergency Recovery Unit. I hovered between life and death for two weeks. Again, my mother and father. Again, the doctors. Again, all the whiteness and the blackness. Again, the pain.

"I wished I would die, even as people kept whispering, over and over, that I had to *want* to live, or there was *no hope* for me.

"When it finally became apparent I would, after all, live, no matter what I wished for and wanted— when I finally regained consciousness and began to recognize people like my parents and the doctors— the shrinks decided that I should get away from the city, and all of its bitter memories, at least for awhile.

"My aunt and uncle had a home in the country. It wasn't a farm, though they did have token horses, cows, chickens, ducks, even a turkey and one pig. They also had grain fields. Wheat, I think. But my uncle wasn't officially 'a farmer.' He was a stock-broker. He hired people to take care of his animals and his fields, like the English gentry hired help.

"My uncle had always liked me. I'd liked his wife and him, too. When I was younger, they used to always have me out to their country place for part of my summers. They and it held fond memories for me. They told my parents to send me along as soon as I was able to travel.

"So, I went to the country. That, in short, tells you how I met up with my cousin, Mark, and be-came sexually involved with him, anally, at a time in my life when I was turned off to vaginal inter-course

"Let me tell you, though, that it was a long, long time before I let even Mark fuck me in the ass. As a matter of fact, we didn't have sex that first summer at all. It was the next year.

"I stayed there that first summer and didn't talk much to anybody. I didn't do much of anything but walk by myself. Everyone seemed to understand, and they made it a point to stay out of my way. I spent days wandering pastures, riding horses, walk-ing the countryside, wading streams. I'd sit off by myself in the shadows of the woods and try desper-ately to forget all that had happened to me in the city to bring me to the country.

"That first summer ended and autumn came. My uncle and aunt moved back to the city. Mark went off to school. I stayed on and continued my days of listless wandering. When winter came, I occasionally went to dinner with the caretaker's family. Usually, though, I'd just curled up by the blazing fire in the main house and read; I did a lot of reading that winter.

"Everything that you're interested in hearing occurred the second summer. The winter passed, the sun returned in all of its full-force heat-producing glory. My aunt, uncle, and cousin returned.

"After having spent so long a time pretty much by myself, I was actually surprised by how excited and happy I was to see them. I kissed them, laughed with them, and even related a few amusing anecdotes as regarded what had happened to me in their absence. I was sure, as were they, that I'd reached, finally, some kind of healthy turning point in my life.

"Mark had grown since I'd last seen him. He had been sixteen the first summer. He was seventeen that second. But there was a world of difference in his complexion, in his physical presence, in his general bearing. He had taken some major steps away from boyhood.

"He was at that ideal age where he could still have fun like a boy, but he had the build and looks of a real man. And by the bulge at his crotch, he'd miraculously sprouted the sexual equipment to match his new-found maturity.

"There had been a time when I had actually thought that all of my sexual drives had been sapped from me by the gang rape. But there was no denying that certain urges were beginning to return that summer. I started remembering some of the sexual *good* times I'd had before the rapes, before the abortion, before all of the pain. Suddenly, I wasn't uncomfortable about my emerging curiosity to see Mark's naked penis and wonder about how it would feel probing my insides.

"Whenever I'd get carried away with such daydreaming of Mark's pecker up my cunt, however, I'd remember that night in the alley. Therefore, I reached a point where I desired Mark to fuck me but, at one and the same time, I was afraid of ever letting him do so.

"Mark and I spent a lot of time together. I'm sure his mother and father had told him to try and do just that. They wanted me to have fun. They wanted to do all that *they* and Mark could to make me forget the horror of what I had gone through. That I felt disloyal to them by coveting their son didn't make me covet him, and what he so obviously had in his pants, any the less.

"Mark and I went to local dances at the country club. We played tennis. We swam. We went riding. We took long walks through the woods.

"Very few people could have spent as much time as we did that summer, done as much as we did together, without the element of sex eventually entering into the picture.

"So what that we were cousins? What in the hell did *that* have to do with the price of tea in China? Try and tell two people, even two first cousins, that they're not in love when love is definitely what they're feeling for each other. In that, yes, I actually thought I was in love with him, and vice versa. And it was a wonderful time and a place for love. It was warm. The butterflies swarmed. The birds sang. The flowers blossomed. Everything was storybook-perfect.

"And when you're nineteen, and your lover is seventeen, love eventually comes to mean *sex*.

"I began to feel those once-thought-completely-lost *stirrings* returning to me. I could tell by the way Mark looked at me, touched me, moved his fingers up the back of my neck and through my hair, by the definite swelling of the already impressive bulge in his pants, whenever he was around me, that he was thinking of sex, also.

"*I* made the first sexual move. I felt that it was my place to do so. Mark was thoroughly familiar with the situation surrounding my being there. He would have never initiated anything himself. He wasn't that kind of guy.

"We were walking through a hay field. It was a good crop that year; the stalks were almost to my waist. We walked into the meadow beyond and came to the edge of a small stream. He picked a flower, a blue-bell, and put it in my hair.

"'I love you,' he said.

"I started to undo my blouse. He watched me, silently. I took off my blouse, unfastened my bra and took it off. Then, I started to unfasten the snap on my skirt. He reached out a hand and stopped me.

"'No,' he said.

"'But I love you, too,' I confessed to him.

"'It's not necessary for you to prove it. Not after what you've been through.'

"I gently shook off his hand and dropped my skirt. He watched me unhitch my panties and add them to my growing pile of discarded clothing. I stood there, naked, in front of him. He eyed me dreamily. I could see the way his cock was extending down the left leg of his pants.

"Slowly, nervously, he began to unbutton his shirt. He took it off. He was blond. His chest was bronzed by the summer sun. He had a muscular, well-defined physique. He had pale-brown dime-sized nipples surrounded by silky haloes of blond hair. He had a wash-board belly. His lower stomach was covered with blond hair that disappeared beneath his pants.

"He unbuckled his belt and unbuttoned his jeans. He slipped off his pants. His Jockey shorts were made impressive by the massive ridge his erection made in them.

"He stood for awhile with just his shorts on. He seemed embarrassed at the stiff state of his cock and by the way a wet spot, caused by his pre-seminal leakage, made his cockhead readily visible beneath the gone-transparent cotton material. I was amused and rather touched by his sudden blush.

"'I do love you,' I said. I went to him. I hugged him and felt his hard dick saying its hello through his under shorts.

"'Jesus, babe,' he said and kissed me. His chest mashed my tits.

"The sun was warm on our bodies.

"I dropped to my knees before him, pulling down his underwear as I did so. My face was right across from his now-freed monster cock that was firmly anchored amidst the golden hair at the base of his belly. His dick's very hugeness suddenly brought back a memory of those even bigger pricks which had gang-raped me in the alley: Negro cocks, all big and instruments-of-pain.

"Mark's boner arched upward to a beautiful pink-red, heart-shaped head. His balls were large, drooping, covered with strands of blond-golden hair. His thighs were hairy. His pubic bush was lush. There was hair across his lower belly that trailed in an ever-thinning fine line upward into that muscular valley parenthesized, on either side, by his marvelously defined pectorals.

"He came down on his knees to join me, grabbing my body to him as he kissed me. I felt his cock hard against my lower belly.

"I resented the unwanted tenseness growing within me, because I wanted him to fuck me, in order to prove to him and to me that I loved him with my whole body, mind, heart, and soul.

"He wanted it, too. He didn't have to say anything. All I had to do was look at and feel the state of his prick. It was hard. It was erect. It was drooling pre-cum. When I reached to wrap as much of it as I could with one hand, it was as if I took hold of a sun-warmed lead pipe.

"'How I've wanted you,' he said. 'How many times I've dreamed of it being just like this.'

"He pushed me onto my back. He climbed on top of me. He worked his fingers between my legs.

"As much as I wanted him, I couldn't get rid of my growing unease. I couldn't get the memory of my rapes out of my mind. Though the day was bright, though I could see that this was Mark and not a raping black man, I couldn't push away the horrible memories that came rushing in to drown me.

"Mark stuck his finger up my cunt. He had large fingers. Each of them was the size of a hard cock.

He worked it inside my snatch. He spread his body out more on top of mine. My titties mushroomed my ribcage. His belly was hard against mine. His prick was stiff between his legs and mine. I could feel his dong dribbling its juice along my inner thigh. I could feel it on its steady move toward the entrance of my vagina. I could feel it arrive and begin its slide inside of me.

"I screamed, and not in pleasure.

"I couldn't help it. And I think Mark must have known that I couldn't help it, because he immediately withdrew what little bit of his prick he'd managed to get into me. He rolled off onto his back and shut his eyes to the glare of the sun.

"'Christ, babe,' he said. 'I knew I shouldn't have even tried, but I just couldn't help myself. If you only knew how much I need me inside you.'

"I was crying. I couldn't help myself. I was bawling not so much because his entry into me had in anyway hurt me physically, but because I really wanted and needed him inside me, too, and didn't know how to let it happen.

"'I shouldn't have tried,' he repeated. 'I shouldn't have, I shouldn't have, I shouldn't have.'

"His cock was still hard. I could tell that he still really wanted me. He started to jack off in substitution. For just a moment, I was tempted to just watch him. There was something sensuous as hell about the way his hand so expertly caressed the length and breadth of his stiff dick.

"Eventually, though, I rolled over and crawled on top of him so that my ass sat his belly. He opened his eyes, and his curious expression asked me what in the hell I was doing. I put my fingers to

114

his lips, in signal that I wanted him to be quiet. I put my fingertips over his eyes and pulled his lids down.

"I lifted myself up slightly so that I was squatting over his crotch. I reached behind and beneath me, slapped away his hand still on his dick, and took hold of his pecker with my own hand. I pulled up his dick so that it was raised perpendicular to his stomach. I fingered the mass of it, rubbing its total length within my fingers.

"Still holding his phallic pole upright, I began to sit my ass down over it so that the top of his dick was suddenly parenthesized by my butt crack.

"Mark didn't say a thing, but I could see his chest heave. His belly went taut. His mouth came open and provided a surprised little gasp of wondrous appreciation.

"His prick was still leaking, and I milked it of more pre-seminal juice. I smeared the natural lubricant over the bulging mass and head of his erection. I moved the tip of his boner to the actual puckered opening of my asshole.

"I'd been fucked in the ass before, but not by my rapists. Butt-fucking still held out pleasant memories for me. As I recalled, it had always felt almost as good as, before my gang-rape, getting prick up front. The guy who had first done it to me had told me he always thought fucking butt was better than sticking it to pussy. Certainly, I wanted it to be better for Mark. I desperately wanted him to have some indication of how I felt for him.

"I shifted my hips to allow the head of his cock to nuzzle my sphincter more intimately. His cockhead actually, finally, pressed on through. My ass walls fell in upon his entering cock corona.

"Mark groaned his appreciation but kept his eyes shut. He brought his hands up to rest on my thighs. He squeezed my legs as if in assurance that he understood and appreciated what I was doing.

"My body dropped down over him, accepting more and more of his thick meat into me. I slid down his monstrous shaft and wondered if I would ever reach the bottom of it. By the time I did, Mark's fingers were clamped even more tightly into my thighs.

"I rested my descended butt upon his muscular belly, his cock completely lost within my spasming asshole. I ground my butt over his stomach muscles, shifting to allow every possible inch of him to push and stir inside me. I reached out a hand, tracing the contours of his body from his neck to his knotted belly button. I then let my fingers wander until they had a handful of his balls. He had such very big nuts.

"I contracted my anal muscles about his dork, squeezing to give him more pleasure. I could tell I succeeded by his groans of pleasure, by the way his mouth opened and shut, by the way his tongue lolled.

"Mark soon began writhing and twisting beneath me, bucking his hips so that his cock moved even more in my asshole. His massive maleness throbbed within me and more firmly pressed into, against, and along my anal walls.

"His ass smashed meadow flowers. There was the smell of their dying within the air. It was sweet, ripe, and wonderful.

"I began riding his phallic pole, slowly. His head rocked from side to side as I did so. I put my palms to his muscular pectorals, held tightly to them, and used them for leverage to help me better move up and down, up and down, up and down over his boner.

"After awhile, we managed a coordinated fucking rhythm.

"I bent my head, and my hair beat his chest. My sphincter scraped his invading pole that slid continuously in and out through it. My cunt leaked an oily pool of wet onto his belly, soon drooled into his belly-button, while his cock continued its leak up my ass.

"Once more, I sat down over his impaling penile spike, the head and neck of which pushed entirely out of sight up my asshole. I ground my ass into his pubic hair, feeling its wiriness scratch my butt. The inside walls of my ass were like a thousand hands, each hand trying separately, and together, to jerk off Mark's wondrous dong.

"I could tell climactic forces were building within him by the way his head and neck flopped uncontrollably from side to side, like a fish out of water. His mouth opened and shut. He groaned. His pelvis thrust upward, always attempting to drive more of himself up and into my anus.

"His cock leaked a steady stream of pre-seminal juice that continued thoroughly to baste my anal insides, making both of our butt-fucking movements more and more smooth and easy.

"My hips lifted, my ass sliding his thick cock shaft to its meaty head. I lowered myself back down along the rigid mass. I bounced more and more frantically on his pole, riding him faster and faster. I just knew that I was bringing him closer and closer to satisfaction. And I, too, was gaining a greater pleasure from the continuing workout his hard cock gave the inside of my rectum.

"Again, I moved up and over his thick-rod penis. I paused at the very summit of his phallic joint and then slid on down. After a few more such slides, Mark could control himself no longer. His body stiffened more. His mouth moved more. His eyes opened and rolled to the back of his head. His hips bucked more. His cock throbbed more.

"It was ejaculation time! His nuts exploded their loads and flooded my butt with hot semen.

"It was—marvel of marvels!—orgasmic for me, too, as gush after gush of his hot sperm exited his dick to light my fire and keep it going."

* * * * * * *

HERE WE HAVE a gang-rape and abortion that leaves a real dread of "normal" sexual intercourse. Yet sex, so much an important part of our natural existence, eventually made our subject strive for the adjustment and compromise that would allow her, somehow, to reincorporate sex back into her life.

Says Robert W. White in *The Abnormal Personality*:

> Following a fright, the overwhelming impulse is simply to avoid the whole frightening situation. Perhaps the danger is so great that no other response is possible. Very often, how-

ever, the danger was only momentary (like a motor accident) or is such that, given a second chance, the person could really cope with it perfectly well. Furthermore, many dangers are incurred in the pursuit of vital interests which the person cannot sacrifice. The pilot whose plane crashes cannot afford to give up his livelihood. The active child does not want to surrender his explorations and adventures because of one occasion he has been frightened.... One has to come to terms with the circumstances of having been frightened. This means acting in direct opposition to the impulse to avoid. It means *renewed contact* with the threat, a *new appraisal* of its threatening character, and *new actions* to cope with it. It means, in short, new learning in the face of a strong motive to avoid new learning.

* * * * * * *

"IT WAS WONDERFUL with Mark that summer. I began to feel the real joys of sex again: sex with a man. Even my nightmares seemed to disappear for nights on end.

"The meadow by the stream became our own special place. We used to go there as often as possible just to be alone with each other, to hear the sounds of the stream, to hear the birds, to lie in the grass, and of course to have sex.

"I loved Mark's strong, hard cock. I loved the way it impressively jutted. I used to kneel between his splayed legs, run my fingers over his thighs, feeling his ropy muscles just below his warm flesh. Then, I'd run my hands through the thick blond bush that clustered the base of his prick. You didn't need a second look to know his cock was the cock of a real man.

"His prick always seemed to know when I planned to go down on it. Its head would turn beet red, and its whole shaft would begin to tremble and jerk. It would spasm, and then his nuts would shift in their sac. At which time, I could always picture all of his thick cream churned to life within his huge, hairy, and testicle-packed scrotum.

"I bent my head forward, licking his cock's belly from its knotted root to its blood-distended head. It tasted deliciously of male and soap. After I'd licked to the top, I went back down the shaft's underbelly again, nuzzling my nose into Mark's pubic hair, pressing my chin into his cum-swollen balls. I loved that smell.

"I kissed his luscious balls, noting how his huge phallus trembled and moved all over the place whenever I did so.

"He wiggled his ass deeper into the meadow grass. His breathing became more hurried and erratic. Now, whenever I touched his cock with my lips, tongue, and/or hands, he would sigh with my caressing.

"I liked just suddenly to grab his cock in my hand and squeeze, watch his big blue phallic veins bulge large and impressive. I liked to lift his nuts, play with them, feel their mysterious heaviness; I wondered how those two gonads of his could possibly manufacture the mess of hot cum they always emptied with such splattering force into my mouth, hand, or asshole.

"Sometimes when I lifted his scrotum, there was enough excessive skin that it flowed sensuously between my fingers.

"I kissed his inner thighs, dragging my lips softly over the almost invisible hair that grew there. Doing so would tickle him, and he would smile. I would stick out my tongue, lick his legs, and feel his thigh muscles jumping with my touch. I'd let my tongue travel back up to his cock, back up to his balls. I'd fill my mouth with saliva.

"He liked me sucking on his balls. I could and really did suck on them, too. I drew them into my mouth, one by one, after my tongue had first washed them clean with spit. They were actually *almost* too much of a mouthful. I would let my cheeks collapse in on them. Mark enjoyed the pain of his nuts mashing.

"I liked to suck his cock, its head passing through my teeth. Looking down his un-submerged monster-cock inches and squeezing them with my hand, I'd watch and savor the experience. I hand-masturbated all of his cock which wasn't in my mouth. I tasted his pre-seminal juice leaked through the cleavage at the top of his pecker. I moved the folds of his loose outer cock flesh up and over his more solid inner cock core.

"I took more of his prick through the gateway of my throat.

"Mark's whole body shivered. His eyes opened wide and watched me go down on him. His watching added to his excitement. He once told me that he was always intrigued by how all of his big cock could *possibly* be taken all of its way up my hungry mouth and throat.

"My lips slid his erection, slipping farther and farther toward its bottom. I sometimes gagged a little, but not usually, and never much. It was almost like his cock was made specifically for my throat. I just let my head keep falling. My eyes watched his belly getting closer and closer. Then, my nose was in his pubic hair and his stiffy was buried completely down my mouth and throat.

"He panted, groaned, and shifted his hips. There was a fire burning in his groin. All of my sucking wasn't putting out that fire, either; it was adding fuel to its flames.

"Once at the bottom, I shifted my head, corkscrewing his prick within my throat. My tongue wrapped his pole and massaged it, feeling the way his thick veins bulged the sides of his shaft. I sucked so hard, he must have thought that I was trying to suck his dick off at its base.

"He writhed, his butt moving from side to side. My tonguing brought him closer and closer to orgasm.

"He put his hands in my hair. He never once tried to force-feed me his pecker, though. He always let me take it on my own sweet time, at my own sweet speed. As physically powerful as he was, as masculine as he was, he was always gentle to and with me. I appreciated that. Because of it, I could love him all the more.

"I pulled my mouth up. My spit slicked the long neck of his dork, and more of it beaded within the strands of his pubic hair at the base of his erection. My lips closed around the lower limits of just his knobby cockhead and fit the groove formed by his circumcision scar.

"Sucking his penis gently, I moved my face back and forth over its shaft, sliding his dick back and forth into and out of my mouth, whipping his dick with my tongue. I increased the intensity of my sucking. I increased the tempo of the rise and fall of my head over his manhood, egging him on toward climax.

"I cupped his testicles, playing with them. One of my hands caressed his thighs and legs.

"Just before he blasted, he bent his legs at their knees and pressed his thighs tightly against my ears. All I could hear were the echoes of my slurps over his phallic lollipop. Then, his thigh muscles tightened all the more, and—even though his legs continue to block my ears—I still heard his screams of climax.

"'Oh, Christ, baby, now, Now, NOW!'

"Then, I really gave a hearty suck in effort to siphon all that delicious cream up from his healthy nuts. His semen tasted like rich and wonderfully runny custard as he cock-fed it to me. Its wet stickiness hung the walls of my throat.

"After he was done and had rested a bit, I let him fuck me up the rear by my going to my hands and knees. He positioned behind me, and I could hear him spit on his hands and rub the saliva over his dong. He put dollops of spit on my pursed sphincter, too, before putting his prick on target.

"It really didn't bother me when his hands ran my thighs to play with the tight lips of my pussy.

"He pushed very gently on his prick positioned at the entrance of my asshole. He kept on pushing until his bulbous cockhead slipped on in, more of his cock doing the same by way of follow-up.

"I jiggled my ass to accommodate all he offered.

"Once in me to his dick's halfway point, he paused and gentlemanly waited for my ass to become comfortable with what it had eaten. Only then did he drive the rest of his awaiting inches home.

"He gave me a series of in and out thrusts and partial withdrawals. Then he, once again, shoved his prick in full depth and left it there while my anal muscles played with it. I wiggled my ass. He groaned. I groaned.

"His fingers took even more liberties with my snatch. He stuck them completely inside me and played with his cock through the thin membrane that separated my asshole from my cunt hole.

"It was a good feeling, having his penis rammed up my butt; his fingers jabbed up my pussy. My torso swung back and forth in my dog-fuck position, my ass over his dong, my cunt over his probing fingers.

"I went wild. My body rocked in orgasm. My head flopped from side to side. My hands grabbed handfuls of grass. I thought I was dying from pleasure.

"Again, he pushed his dick in all the way. His fingers jabbed deeply up my cunt.

"He fucked and fucked, holding back his own orgasm for as long as he could. That long prick of his worked my ass like sixty.

"No man, though, could put off the inevitable forever, because my ass was damned tight. Each pull and push of his dork, through and inside of it, stripped his meat all the closer to blast-off.

"He slobbered on my neck. He mumbled something low and purr-like.

"We became one trembling mass on the grass as his cock puked wad after wad of viscid spunk and my ass accepted it, one and all. The meadow filled with our groans of pleasure, our wet flesh's smacks and sucks, and our howl-like cries of ecstasy. We drowned out the birds, the stream, and the wind through the trees, as wave after wave of ecstasy cascaded through us.

"Those were the days, my friend. Such goddamned beautiful, wonderful days! Nothing could have been better for me. I thank God that there was someone, like Mark, there at the right time, at the right place, even if he *was* my cousin.

"Then, the day came that I shall never forget, in that it was really such an important milestone day for me.

"It started just like any other of our days together. We had gone to the meadow by the stream. I had sucked off his peter and had rolled to my belly in the grass. Only this time, he turned me over on my back. I didn't think too much of it, because sometimes he liked to take my ass that way: my lifting my legs, his cock going into my rectum while we were face-to-face. That's what I thought he was planning to do.

"I wasn't too surprised, either, when he did a lot of foreplay kissing and caressing before initiating our actual butt-fuck. That sort of thing really turned us both on, really made us both hot to trot.

"He ran his fingers down my thighs, pried open my legs. He stuck his fingers in my cunt and stroked my clitty. As I've said, I had, by then, long-since passed the point of being afraid of his hand up my snatch. I could let him do it and actually enjoy it. So, he jabbed his fingers on in, deeper and deeper, running the sides of his hand against my erect clit. I just shut my eyes and let him have at it. I was enjoying every moment.

"His tongue wandered my tits, down my neck, down my belly. Then, it went back up my belly, licking at one of my nipples. His tongue massaged, and he bit. After my teat's nippled center went nicely taut, he went on over to my other nipple and did the same.

"All the while, his hands continued to caress my vagina, dipping in and out of my honey pot. He washed his hands in the exotic juice oozing from my pussy.

"I opened my legs wider, allowing him to kneel between them, allowing him to look closer at my cunt while he hand-fucked it. He eased my legs wider. As he did so, my twat gaped, allowing torrents of retained juice to exit and slide the crack of my ass. His face dragged down my belly. He stuck his tongue through the doorway of my vagina and drank the wetness he found there.

"He located the erect button of my clit, swollen as it was like a miniature prick. He battled it with his tongue, working his face in closer so that he could even bite it.

"My hips pushed upward so that his nose, mouth, and eyes, disappeared in my muff hair. I pulled my legs shut around his ears, bouncing frantically as I tried to achieve orgasm on his French-kissing tongue.

"He ate my snatch until I orgasmed. After which, I opened my eyes and saw him still between my legs. He held his prick in one hand and spread it with a veneer of my pussy juice and his spit and pre-seminal slime.

"He fell forward on top of me. His chest was muscular. His cock was large and hard, nestled in my pubic hair. I let my legs rise about his waist. His hands moved his cock to my tightly muscled ass-hole.

"He dragged his penis head back and forth along the crease of my butt, leaving a trail of his pre-seminal juice wherever his dick went.

"I don't know just when he made his decision to stick his cock up my snatch, instead of up my ass. He told me later that it wasn't pre-planned; it just was one of those spontaneous moments.

"He did *start* pressing his dick up my ass. I did *feel* the hugeness of his heart-shaped cockhead nuzzling its way through my sphincter. But suddenly, his cock wasn't at my asshole any longer; it was at my cunt. And it was slipping on in. All of its hard, delicious inches were sliding into my miraculously, marvelously unresisting snatch. The strange part being that I was relaxed all of the time he was doing it, even after I realized what he was doing. Suddenly, I wanted him and his dick, both, just where they were.

"His penis kept right on going, managing a complete insertion in one long and easy movement. I responded by heaving up my welcoming hips and grinding my pelvis into his. It felt so wonderful to have a thick and friendly cock, again, buried to manly balls within me. I'd been so long without the sensation that it was only then and there that I fully realized how much I'd been missing.

"'Jesus,' I moaned. And I somehow suspected that there *should have been* discomfort and displeasure. But all there was—was the joy. I was flooded with it. My body was awash in it.

"While I was still engrossed in the miracle taking place, he pulled up, dragging inch after inch of his hard cock over my swollen clitoris. He then slipped his prick down again, my cunt lips finally gumming the root of his dork. Our pubic hair met, entwined, and he twisted his prick deep inside me.

"I gagged on my pleasure. I tried to formulate something to say, but I couldn't.

"There was no pain, no blood, and no discomfort. For once, in ever so long, I was experiencing the same combination of wonderful sensations that had been possible for me before I'd been deprived of them, for so long, by having been gang-raped. It was good to renew my acquaintance with those passions, as if I were discovering long-lost friends.

"Suddenly, I seemed a born-again sexual creature.

"Mark didn't take but a few pumps of his cock up my snatch before I orgasmed for the first time on it. Before he was finished blasting his cum up my snatch, though, I lost count of how many times I climaxed over and around his skillfully pussy-maneuvering penis.

"After awhile, it seemed I was exploding non-stop, no pauses in between. It was pure bliss. It was enjoyment supreme. It was the kind of sex people usually only read about.

"One after another, after another, those moments of sheer joy convulsed me. Just as one climax ended, another began, even sometimes overlapping the one before it; I was thrust to higher and higher plateaus of pleasure and wonder.

"Mark just kept on fucking and fucking and fucking, while I just kept climbing, and climbing, and climbing to new heights of orgasmic bliss. No matter how high I went, too, there was always one more thrust or withdrawal of his cock to send me bounding to yet another higher pinnacle.

"My body writhed and convulsed, beneath his penile stabbing, until I was too tired and exhausted to writhe and convulse any longer.

"Finally, Mark blasted, and I didn't know, until that moment, that drowning in man-spunk could be so totally breath-taking, marvelously wondrous, and multiple-climax triggering."

* * * * * * *

ADJUSTMENT BY OUR SUBJECT was made. A compromise was achieved whereby she finally found herself psychologically able, once again, to return to sex of the kind made long time abhorrent by traumatic past experiences.

State Thorpe and Katz in *The Psychology of Abnormal Behavior*:

> Some emotionally disturbed individuals show their maladjustments in sexually aberrant behavior. This behav-

ior includes all sexual acts in which gratification is obtained by practices other than the socially approved method of heterosexual intercourse (coitus). Deviations in sexual behavior may result from various physical and psychological influences or a combination of both. Clinical research shows, however, that the vast majority of such deviations, whether they are moderate or extreme, are the result of psychological factors.

That sexual rape is traumatic cannot be denied. But multiple rapes, plus an unwanted pregnancy, and a necessitated abortion, were bound to have multiplied the trauma for our subject. At first, the result was her rejection of sex entirely, with an accompanying retreat into physical isolation—without sex—for a long length of time. As immediate memories of her traumatic and painful episodes began to pale, however, sexual release again became important, especially when Mark's appearance on the scene made such stirrings more conveniently and safely realized.

That Mark was a relative was probably of great advantage to our subject's rehabilitation. Since there was a familial bond between the two, they were allowed to achieve an immediate closeness, with accompanying sense of "safeness," which the woman would probably not have allowed herself with an outsider. That theirs was a mutual attraction, and that Mark was gentle and understanding in his approach to and advantaging of it, only assisted the healing process.

The subject of this case history had what Thorpe and Katz would probably describe as a *transient disorder*: one which rose as a means of struggling to adjust to the horror of what occurred in the alley and at the hospital. Anal love was utilized as a substitute for normal intercourse; incest—in this particular instance—accidental rather than planned.

Expound Thorpe and Katz:

> ...some individuals manifest reaction patterns that are more or less transient in character and that appear to be an acute symptom response to a situation.... Sometimes the symptoms are the immediate means used by the individual in his struggle to adjust to an overwhelming situation.... A condition may be regarded as a transient situational personality disorder if a recession of all behavior symptoms occurs when the situational stress diminishes or is no longer present.... Under conditions of great or unusual stress, the normal personality may utilize defensive patterns of reaction to deal with overwhelming fear.... In any event, the person returns to his normal state within a matter of weeks or at the most a few months after the situational stress has been removed.

The subject today is a happily married house-wife with three children. She recalls all of the horrors of her gang-rape, pregnancy, and abortion, with clarity, but she has adjusted to them all and has long-since moved on.

Allan Fromme, in his *Ability to Love*, states:

> Even a damaging experience can have its positive results. We cannot plan what is best for us in every detail of our lives, and even if we knew what was best we could not always bring it to pass in the way we dream.

IV.

HOMO RELATIONS

"**IT WAS INEVITABLE** that Adrian and I get together and fuck. Not because we were same-sex cousins—though, genetically, that probably had a lot to do with it—but because we looked so much alike and, as a direct result of that (narcissism run rampant?!), we really were turned on by each other. Even if we had both been straight, we would have likely managed some bit of homosexual experimentation, in that we were both adventuresome in our explorations of potential sexual fun and games.

"In every man, I think, there is a bit of self-love. It's fascinating to have sex with someone who is almost your exact duplicate, without being an official twin. It's kind of like fucking, or making love, to a magic mirror that responds in kind.

"The two of us were drawn to each other from the very beginning, rather like yin and yang. We lived in the same neighborhood—our houses only a couple of blocks away. We went to the same school. We even went to the same church on Sundays.

"Everyone who didn't know we were cousins thought we were twins. And it was always fun to

133

play those twin games that twins invariably play. We often changed girls mid-date, just to see if either girl could tell the difference. And, yes, we did both date girls and did enjoy them.

"Adrian and I were like two peas in the same pod. We did the same things, went to the same places. We even participated in the same sports. Both of us turned out for tennis, soccer, and gymnastics. One year, we were co-captains of both the tennis and gymnastics teams.

"Being in so many sports events, we saw a lot of each other in the locker room. We saw a lot of each other stripped down stark naked.

"It was always sexually exciting to look at his body, knowing that his was pretty much the same reflection that greeted me every time I looked into a mirror.

"Although when you came right down to it, there were a few minor differences. His cock was a fraction of an inch longer than mine. I'm confident enough of my manhood, and always have been, to admit to that. Our circumcision scars were, also, different where they circled the respective coronas of our peckers. And, he had a small heart-shaped mole on his left ass cheek; I didn't.

"There was a lot of fooling around between us that went on in the locker room. From simple grab ass, to feeling each other's dong, to an occasional fuck behind the lockers or in the towel room. It was all part of growing up, and we never looked upon any of it as being particularly wrong or dirty. We were just doing what two horny guys did naturally.

"Thrown together in the sporty-sweaty atmosphere and comradeship of competitive sports, nude male bodies on each and every side of us, it didn't seem strange to either of us that sex should happen, easily and no-nonsense.

"Considering all the times we had sex with our other team mates and/or with each other in the locker room, I always thought it strange that neither Adrian nor I had our *first* fuck-together homosexual experience there.

"Our first time was when our two families went camping. My family owned this large plot of virgin timber in Washington State and, in the summers, we all did a lot of camping there. On one of those trips, Adrian and I decided that we would take our sleeping bags, leave the cabin, and go sleep under the stars. It was a beautiful and warm evening.

"We piled some loose pine needles near a big pine tree and spread out our sleeping bags. Then for the longest time, we didn't say anything. We just looked up at that crystal-clear night sky and listened to the sounds of the forest all around us. Then all of a sudden, 'it' just happened.

"That was the beginning. Here we are, all these years later, and we are still together and still doing it. We now have an apartment that we share, making it even more convenient for sucking and fucking one another whenever the mood hits us.

"That first time, I was the one who was first to ass-fuck. I'm the more anal; Adrian prefers to suck cock and/or get his meat eaten.

"I'm not sure why I'm so into male ass (figuratively and literally). I had this shrink talk to me about it once. I thought maybe it was because I once saw my brother fuck his girl friend in the ass. I do have a brother, by the way: older. He looks nothing like me. As a matter of fact, I think my brother is a bit plain looking. But, then, maybe, I'm bias? He has had his share of girls in his life, so they obviously look more favorably on his looks than I do. I mean, the thought never even—*not once*—crossed my mind, like it always had with cousin Adrian, that we should ever get together for some butt-fucking and cock-sucking.

"Back to seeing Peter—that's my brother's name, by the way—butt-fuck his girl friend, I remember that mom and dad weren't home at the time. They'd gone somewhere for the whole weekend. I wasn't really supposed to be home, either. I was supposed to be spending the weekend with Adrian, but Adrian had come down with the stomach flu.

"I was upstairs in bed, playing with *my* peter, when my *brother* Peter came home with his girl. I heard them laughing and talking. Rather than go down, to let them know they had company, I just stayed put. Always a bit of a voyeur, though, I quickly decided to peek at them; so, I crept out into the hallway and leaned down into the stairwell.

"I was surprise to find it so dark downstairs. There was only one light on in the living room, the blinds pulled shut.

"I heard Peter asking—I think her name was June—whether he might fuck her. I remember her saying that she was having her period, and that she couldn't, or wouldn't. Then Pete said it was okay, because he could fuck her in her ass, instead. They both had a good giggle about that, after which she— color me shocked as hell at the time!—gave her consent.

"I was fascinated when they both stripped. As I said, I've never found my brother, clothed or naked, physically attractive, and that time was no exception, but his having a female stark naked, right with him, did pique my interest.

"I *do* admit to Peter having an impressive cock and balls. At the time, I was a tad envious. Also, I was jealous by how his chest and belly had such decided muscle definition with hair around his cock, on his chest, underneath his arms, on his legs, and up the crease of his ass. By comparison, I was skinny and hairless, my balls hardly dropped.

"June got down on her hands and knees, her upper body positioned over the seat cushions of the couch. It looked to me as if that wasn't her first time with dick due for sticking up her poop-shoot.

"Peter, his dick pink and hard, got down behind her. He spit in both of his hands and smeared his saliva over the shaft of his dick. His pecker looked all glassy and shiny after he'd thoroughly basted it.

"He spit on his fingers again, spread open the cheeks of June's ass and wet her anal pucker with a big sticky gob of mucus. Then, he aimed his spitty spear right on her spitty target.

"'Try being a bit more careful, this time, jock,' June said. 'The last time, you almost killed me.'

"I knew right then and there that I had been right about Peter's cock having been shoved up her butt before the then and there.

"He leaned on over her. I was positioned so that I got a good side view of everything that was happening. I could see his cock pushing through her asshole. As he was pressing home, he placed both of his hands on her ass and spread her rear-end cheeks nice and wide.

"When his cock was well on its way to full submersion, he let his hands move from her butt to her tits which were mushroomed on the couch. He started playing with her jugs. She lifted a bit so that her titties hung into his hands like two giant tear drops. He really massaged them, and I could tell she really liked what he was doing fore *and* aft.

"He rammed his cock into her farther. His balls audibly slapped against her ass. One of his hands moved from her tits to rest, palm-down, against her overhanging belly.

"He made his first official out-and-return pump of her hole.

"'Jesus, that feels so good, honey,' he mumbled. 'That just feels so damned, damned, damned good.'

"He proceeded to pump her some more, in smooth and easy out-and-in movements. He kept his one hand busy squeezing away at a milky tit.

"He lowered his mouth to the crease of her neck and shoulder. He kissed and then bit her.

"Their bodies moved into a well-coordinated fucking rhythm. They started moaning and groaning. And as he kept on pushing and pulling his rod into and out of her, I felt my own little (at the time) pecker growing hard between my legs. I watched as he squeezed her tit so that the flesh of her boob, like Crisco, ballooned out through his gripping fingers.

"With each of his thrusts, I watched his nads flop against her ass like a couple of those wrecking balls used to knock down buildings. A few times, he would pull his prick out of her so far that I could see his circumcision scar running around the base of his massive cockhead.

"In and out his dick went, faster and faster. Each of his plunges brought a groaning from her lips. His body quivered. He grunted loudly. One time, all of the way fucked into her, he stopped all movement. For an instant, I thought he was stuck, like a guy dog sometimes gets his dick stuck in a bitch, needing a splash of cold water to get him unhooked. I even looked in the direction of the upstairs bathroom, wondering if there was a pail handy.

"'Easy, baby, easy,' he said finally. 'I'm almost there. I almost couldn't stop myself that time. Honey, I'm just *that* close.'

"The two stayed frozen like statues for the longest time. Then, finally, my brother's dick started moving again.

"I just watched, fascinated as all hell by the sight of his hard cock, attached to his body, running its whole length back and forth, out and in, of her asshole. His ass cheeks dimpled each and every time his hips shoved forward to bury his prick home.

"He kept up the steady humping. They kept up their combined moaning and groaning and grunting. They turned all glossy with sweat.

"'Good, baby, good,' he complimented in a guttural mutter. 'That is so Jesus-fucking good.'

"Suddenly, I realized that while he was downstairs shoving his cock to her asshole, I was upstairs fingering my pecker. Every time he shoved his cock home, my hand slid way down over my meat. Every time he pulled almost free, my hand slipped up to my cockhead.

"My whole body was starting to shiver with the pleasure. Oh, I'd played with myself before, plenty of times, but this was the first time I'd gotten quite *as much* pleasure out of the playing.

"June began to cry out, 'Peter, Peter, Peter.' I could see her ass really start to move under the continuing onslaught of his battering-ram dork. It was really something to see, let me tell you.

"Then Peter's hips really started going wild. His cock plugged in and out so fast that I could hardly keep time beating on my own prick. He just kept going, going, and going. Every time his belly whacked loudly against her naked ass, there was a wet *smacking* sound.

"'Holy God, I'm coming!' he yelled loudly. 'Jesus, holy fucking shit!'

"He rammed his shiny dork into her gripping asshole, mating his lower belly with her buns, and left it there.

"After that, I wasn't too sure what happened, because I was dealing with a handful of my own exploded cum. Granted, there wasn't too much of it, but there was enough. That was the first time my cock had actually spit semen.

"I took my scant bit of semen with me back to my bedroom and wiped it off on a Kleenex. Then I climbed under my blankets. Feeling mighty fine, I fell asleep.

"The next morning, I thought I'd dreamed it all. But when Peter discovered that I had been in my room, during all that time he'd been ass-fucking June, he got all strange and nervous. That, and the cum-crusted Kleenex I kept as a souvenir for a long time, told me it had been real all right.

"So, maybe it was that particular butt-plugging scenario which somehow contributes, today, to my fascination with all things asshole. There was something so exceptionally erotic about Peter's swollen prick pressing in and out of June, of his erupting his cum into her butt at the same time my own cock puked sperm into my hand for the very first time. I know one thing that isn't two: I never get the same kind of thrill out of any sex that *doesn't* somehow involve an asshole. That's probably why I'm so into homosexuality. Bun-fucking, after all, is one of the prime ways of getting off your rocks when you're queer, right?

"Since Adrian isn't all that much into ass, male or otherwise, I don't know why he still gets off so well and so often with me. You'll have to ask him.

"No denying that Adrian enjoys male mouth wrapping his pecker and isn't averse to sucking a bit of cock himself. No denying that I enjoy my mouth wrapping his pecker, too, especially when he's simultaneously munching my dick. No denying, though, that I far prefer fucking his ass or getting fucked in the ass by him.

"By the way, it's not because I fear women that I'm a homosexual. Frankly, I have nothing against women and have successfully fucked any number of them.

"In college, Adrian and I belonged to the same fraternity. After all the big sports events, there were invariably two or three prostitutes brought to the house to be passed around for fucking. And even then, while I got no whoopee-wow pleasure out of sticking my cock up cunt, neither did I have any trouble doing it. I could stick my prick up a vagina, and I could climax there as easily as could the best heterosexual stud in our house (that would have been Max Menlaw). No big deal! Nor should you assume that I derive no pleasure from pussy-fucks, because I did and do. It's all a matter, I guess, of degree of pleasure. I do not get, nor have I ever gotten, nearly as much pleasure from plugging vagina as from plugging ass.

"In the same respect, however, I do not get as much enjoyment out of fucking a female's asshole as I do from fucking the asshole of some guy. And I have fucked my share of female ass. During those college orgies, if the prosties were occupied with prick up their fronts, there was no stigma attached to any of us going up behind for a bit of shit-stirring. Certainly, even then, I preferred screwing a woman's ass to screwing her cunt, and I made it a point to do just that as often as possible.

"I realized quite early that I was, perhaps, overly infatuated with ass—especially with male ass. Because of this, and because I came to think of myself as a very liberal-minded individual, I made it a point to experience as many diverse sexual experiences as possible. In short, that merely means that I made it a point to fuck female cunt, ass, and mouth, as well as male ass and mouth. I also made it a goal to get sucked by both men and women, to eat out both men and women. There was even a time, at a picnic, when three of us guys simultaneously fucked a watermelon. There was another time when I fucked a dog: not a two-legged one, either. Doggy breath very bad and a decided turn-off, by the way!

"And of all those myriad types of sexual activity in which I participated, I achieved orgasms in varying degrees of pleasure. Out of the total, I came to the conclusion that I received more enjoyment when ass, decidedly male ass, played a predominant or supporting role.

"That's not to say that the time might not arise when I finally will find an exception. That's, also, not to say that I am not still continually looking for that exception.

"Though Adrian and I might be considered lovers, we do not limit ourselves sexually to just each other. We both agree that would be ridiculous, especially since he's also almost exclusively into, figuratively and literally, pussy. However, Adrian and I do continue to have sex with each other on a regular basis.

"I find ridiculous any notion of incest being bad in our case. Incest only became a taboo in effort to prevent the birth of idiots, through inbreeding, and there won't be any children, retards or otherwise, from Adrian and me fucking and sucking.

"You might find it interesting that my anal fixation and enjoyment aren't limited entirely to my being the active partner, either. I receive pretty much the same degree of satisfaction from having cock inserted up my bum as in putting my dick fast and furious to someone else's asshole. I have this ability to orgasm with just a hard dick massage of my prostate and anal canal, no manipulation of my penis even necessary. My first indication that ejaculation was possible for me in this way was with Adrian's *very first* fuck of my ass.

"I fucked him first on that camping trip I told you about, him and me out under the stars. After I'd done fucking him, though, I obligingly rolled immediately to my belly to allow him some *give as got*. He didn't have to be invited twice.

"He rubbed his prick down with spit and inserted it between my buns. With a steady pressure, he heaved his thickness into my hole. The insertion was accompanied by a sunburst of pleasure that radiated throughout my whole body.

"From the moment of his cock's actual submersion into me, things began to happen.

"I received a great joy from the mere press of his muscular body atop me.

"I thrilled at the way his large nipples dug into my back, the way his balls dragged the slope of my offered-up ass.

"There was something aphrodisiacal about the smell of our combined sweat.

"My anal walls collapsed to smother his prodding erect dong. Each of his ensuing thrusts pushed me into a universe of enjoyment, pleasure, and sensations I'd never before experienced.

"My muscles knotted, my butt spasmed, and I groaned with the sheer wonder of having my ass fucked by my cousin's huge and sexy dick. I almost choked on the sheer intensity of my pleasure.

"Adrian, too, was caught up in the ass-fuck. He gave me a series of powerful strokes that jammed me completely full of his throbbing pecker. He pulled back to his cockhead and paused for only a fraction of a second before giving me all of his cock again. His balls banged sensuously against my upturned butt.

"He grunted his exertion. His sweaty belly ground my butt's twin mounds.

"He wrapped his hands about my body, his fingers caressing my nipples as his hips continued to make his cock do wonderful things up my asshole.

"Adrian knew just the right things to do and did them. He *still* does them.

"His thrusts were evenly paced, as were his withdrawals. Never did he seem exceptionally frantic or hurried.

"His dick continually rammed my prostate. His prick was so long and so thick that every thrust, every withdrawal, drug his fat cockhead and inches of dick over my sensitive anal glad. It was wild.

"The fuck was long and easy, Adrian somehow enduring the tightness of my anus without succumbing to premature ejaculation. Later, I discovered that, unbeknownst to me, his balls had previously blasted while I'd fucked him, so it wasn't as if he'd come to my ass with his nuts completely full.

"His chest and belly were molded to my back. One of his cheeks rested against one of mine. His pelvis rocked on my ass, his cock moving within my rectum.

"I became more and more excited when, judging by the intensity of Adrian's panting and by the increasing momentum of his fuck, I knew that he was on the verge of climax. I longed for the feel of his hot fluid jettisoning up my bowels.

"I had a new and even more powerful surge of enjoyment in the pit of my stomach. It swept out to stiffen every muscle of my body. I bit my lip so hard that I tasted the saltiness of my blood. I felt this intensely thrilling sensation getting stronger and stronger within me.

"All the while, Adrian fucked his cock back and forth through the clutching corridor of my hole.

"'I'm coming,' he finally whispered in my ear. 'I'm coming, coming, coming.'

"His words heralded my own orgasm as well. My cock spit great gobs of goo to paste the sleeping bag beneath my grinding belly.

* * * * * * *

ACCORDING TO THORPE AND KATZ in *The Psychology of Abnormal Behavior*, there are four types of sexuality. They are:

1. The individual's tendencies are always homosexual, regardless of opportunities for heterosexual relations.
2. Where there are opportunities for both heterosexual and homosexual relations, the individual prefers heterosexual relations at one time, homosexual at another.
3. Where there are opportunities for both heterosexual and homosexual relations, the individual engages in heterosexual relations only; but where no opportunities for heterosexual relations are available...the individual engages in homosexual activities.
4. Under all conditions in which heterosexual opportunities may or may not be available, the indi-

vidual engages only in heterosexual activities.

Ted and Adrian, in this case history, seem to
suggest two other categories. Ted would most likely
come under a modification of Thorpe and Katz's
number two. While he would prefer homosexual relations all the time, he will often select sex with the
opposite sex for pure variety. On the other hand,
Adrian would fall under a different modification of
the same number two. While he would prefer heterosexual relations (excepting his homosexual contact with his cousin), he often selects to have sex
with the *same* gender for a bit of variety.

David Reuben, in his *Everything You Always
Wanted to Know About Sex*, states:

> Total sexual stimulation is a means
> of intensifying sexual pleasure by util-
> izing all the available erotic pathways
> to reinforce and add to the cumulative
> gratification of the sexual experiences.
> Every available sensory pathway is re-
> cruited, first consciously, later almost
> automatically, to enhance sexual suc-
> cess.

Nor should the fact that both of the men, in our case
study, are indulging in sex with both males and females seem so extraordinary.

Kinsey, Pomeroy, and Martin, in their *Sexual
Behavior in the Human Male*, add:

There are individuals in the population whose histories are exclusively homosexual both in experience and psychic relations. But the record also shows that there is a considerable portion of the population whose members have combined within their individual histories, both homosexual and heterosexual experiences and/or psychic response. There are some whose heterosexual experiences predominate, there are some whose homosexual experiences predominate, there are some who have quite equal amounts of both types of experiences.

Nor, for that matter, should one necessarily criticize the choices for sex as made by our two cousins in this case study.

As state Thorpe and Katz:

[The sexually happy person is] he or she who does not feel sex is dirty, who does not have fears about it, who accepts it as part of nature and of human nature and a natural source of pleasure. It is a person who is interested in sex, appreciates it, enjoys it.

Probably, Ted wasn't that far off when he said that it was inevitable that he and Adrian get together. That they so closely physically resembled each other might well have been enticement enough. The incestuous barrier—which is probably the

greatest preventative barrier to the sexual relationship of twins—was a rather vague and far removed
factor in this particular less-immediate blood-line
instance. Ted and Adrian were, likewise, able to re-
ject the incest taboo on the basis that such taboo was
originally formulated for prevention of inbreeding
among blood-related males and females.

States Robert M. Goldenson in *The Encyclopedia of Human Behavior*:

> At one time…prohibitions [of in-
> cest] were attributed to the dangers of
> inbreeding, but today this theory is
> largely discredited because it applies
> only when there are latent hereditary
> defects in the family line. A more
> widely accepted explanation is that in-
> cest creates rivalries that disrupt family
> life and prevent the society from
> enlarging and strengthening itself
> through outside relations.
>
> The prevalence of incest taboos in-
> dicates that the urge to form these rela-
> tionships must be widespread.

For anyone with even the slightest homosexual in-
clination, what enticement to make love to/with
your mirror-image!

Dr. Allen Fromme, in his *Ability to Love*, further
expounds:

> Through the years—infancy, child-
> hood, adolescence—the lover is devel-
> oping his self-image, creating an iden-

tity for himself. He tries on a variety of
identities as he goes along; hence the
daydreaming of which we spoke ear-
lier. He looks for models in history,
story books, and in the world around
him. He develops crushes on teachers,
athletic coaches, older friends, school
heroes and heroines. His first...attach-
ment is still primarily an expression of
his attachment to himself. As we shall
see in our exploration of romantic love,
the lover at first loves his own image of
the beloved, not the beloved....

It is, perhaps, easier to see how the two might have
been attracted to each other sexually than it is to ac-
count for Ted's preference towards homosexuality.
Thorpe and Katz state:

Some investigators have considered
homosexuality as an inborn behavior
pattern; others have assumed that the
condition is caused by hormonal im-
balance. Most researchers and clini-
cians explain the development of homosexuality on the basis of psychological factors: conditioning and adjustment. They consider homosexuality
to be the result of environmental experiences and emotional stress.

Perhaps Ted was right in assuming that his witness-
ing of his brother's anal confrontation with June

was a contributing factor to a later preference for anal sex specifically and homosexual sex in general.

After all, as states Robert W. White in *The Abnormal Personality*:

> The simplest psychogenic explanation of homosexuality would be that the person becomes fixated upon this object choice because of gratification happening in childhood or early adolescence.

And Dr. Sigmund Freud, in his *Basic Writings*, has similar observations:

> The most striking process of puberty has been selected as its most characteristic; it is the manifest growth of the external genitals which have shown a relative inhibition of growth during the latency period of childhood.... A most complicated apparatus has thus been formed for future use.
>
> This apparatus can be set in motion by stimuli, and observation teaches that the stimuli can effect it three ways: from the outer world through the familiar erogenous zones; from the inner organic world by ways still to be investigated; and from the psychic life, which merely represents a depository of external impressions and a receptacle of inner excitations.

* * * * * * *

"YOU MIGHT, I SUPPOSE, think of Adrian and me as bisexuals: Adrian probably more so than I, because, when he's not fucking around with me, he *prefers* snatch. Of course, everything depends upon one's definition of bisexuality. And that can get pretty sticky.

"Unlike many homosexuals, I don't limit myself exclusively to male-male sex. Unlike many heterosexuals, Adrian doesn't limit himself exclusively to male-female sex. Neither of us, even though we each *do* have a particular sexual preference, want to get stuck in a sexual rut.

"I think Adrian and I have very healthy attitudes as regards sex. I think it is partially due to our upbringing. We both came from relatively wealthy parents who had a broad-minded attitude about life in general. They did not hide sex or knowledge of sex from us. Nor did they make us think that it was something dirty.

"Our whole lives have been geared toward doing what is enjoyable.

"Certainly, my preference for anal sex did not derive from any fear of getting some girl pregnant. All the girls I knew were as well acquainted with contraceptives as I was. Our parents were anxious for us to practice it. There was, therefore, no fear on my part of ever likely fathering a bastard.

"You know, a lot of the girls I bring back to the apartment, these days, often like anal intercourse, even if I pick them up figuring to fuck their cunts, eat their snatches, or have them give me blow-jobs.

Perhaps there is something to that old adage about like attracting like.

"The other evening, I went to an art show put on by a homosexual friend of mine. While I was there, I met this girl who knew friends of mine living in Los Angeles. We struck up a conversation, sexual interest, and I invited her back to my place, where we had a couple of drinks and proceeded, from there, to the bedroom.

"She took off her dress and panties. I stripped down completely, and then helped her off with her bra that had become snagged. Once her bra was off, and her large tits hung free, we added that last bit of underwear to the growing pile on the chair.

"Her name was Suzy. When I pulled her to me, her large mammary glands mashed against my chest. I kissed her neck, kissed her tits. I found her nipples, kissed them, bit them, felt them erecting beneath my playfulness.

"I dropped to my knees, rubbing my tongue over her firm belly en route to her snatch. I wrapped my arms around her, gripped her buns firmly and pulled her pelvis to me.

"I buried my face into the crinkly tangle of her pubic hair. I pressed my tongue between her cunt lips. Her snatch was wet. I tasted her ripe fish-oil juiciness and licked her twat.

"She groaned her appreciation, took a firmer stance on the floor, and revolved her hips sensuously. She put her hands on my shoulders.

"I continued to tongue-fuck her, realizing that I was giving her pleasure though experiencing little physical enjoyment myself. I did not, however, find eating her hole distasteful. There was a certain degree of mental enjoyment I derived from the realization that she was getting off on my oral caresses.

"She moved her hands from my shoulders to my head, put her fingers into my hair, and pushed my mouth even more firmly against her twat. I opened my mouth wider, folded my lips forward over my teeth, pressed into her mons and gently munched.

"Her hips jerked. She bent her legs at the knees, slipping down to the floor to join me, making sure all the while, that my mouth was not disturbed in its nibbling of her twat.

"I continued eating her out until I was sure she'd achieved at least two orgasms. Then, I moved my tongue up her belly to her tits. I worked my teeth around one nipple for a couple of minutes, and then I kissed my way her neck to her lips.

"She fell completely back on the floor.

"'Fuck me,' she whispered.

"Since I was already pretty much laid out on top of her, my cock didn't have to go far to be on the target area nestled within her pubic hair. My prick was erect and ready to go. One of my hands felt for the entrance to her snatch and to guide my penis to that opening. She opened her legs wider.

"I placed my cock to the mouth of her sex-cavity. I pressed the head of my dick through the guarding portals, feeling vaginal muscles clamping down hard. Then, as I brought both hands back to her tits, I massaged her jugs while I rammed the rest of my dork into her. When I did that, her legs sprung upward, her ankles locking to the small of my back. Her body thrust upward in effort to take even more of my dick into her.

"While my cock was working at her cunt, I pushed my tongue into her mouth. We exchanged spit. While kissing has never given me any great satisfaction, I have long been aware that there are many people who do enjoy it; she was one.

"Her cunt continued to work on and over my prick. Her vaginal lips and muscles chewed on my pecker. It was like a vacuum down there, between her legs, attempting to yank my cock off where it anchored to my lower belly.

"I proceeded to push and pull my cock, seeing that my prick rubbed against or battered her swollen clit as often as was possible. I varied my angle of attack so that my cock explored each and every inch of her sex hole.

"Her body spasmed beneath me with the pleasure my fucking was giving her. She bit my neck. More juice flooded about my penis. Her hips started grinding her pubic hair into mine. All the while, I used long, steady strokes to pump my pecker inside her.

"I was not without some degree of enjoyment. My penis was being masturbated by her vaginal muscles. I was receiving signals that told me I was preparing for ejaculation.

"Her body again convulsed against me. I again enjoyed satisfaction in knowing that *she* was orgasming and that my penis was the cause of it. Sucking sounds came from our bodies, echoing from our points of contact, *smacking* where our sweaty bellies met and then pulled apart.

"I worked my hands beneath her back, gliding them down to grip her ass and pull her more fully over my dick. Upon doing this, she orgasmed again.

She screamed out her joy, scratching my shoulders as she did so. She bit my neck.

"At this point, I knew I could push myself over into an orgasm, too. So, I gave her the remaining thrusts necessary and gushed my seminal fluid from me to her guts.

"Her thigh muscles tightened about my waist. Her vagina fluttered around my exploding dick.

"My shooting complete, I went into automatic after-play, knowing that most any woman is apt to be slower to fall from her sexual heights than a male is. I left my cock inside her, massaged her ass with my hands. I licked at her tits, and then kissed her neck, her cheeks, her eyes, and her mouth.

"'Your cock is still hard, Mr. Stud,' she whispered when we ended the kiss.

"'Damned if you're not right.'

"'Stick it up my butt, baby. Stick it up while it's still all wet with your cum and with my cunt's own juicy lubricant.'

"That's exactly what she said.

"As I lifted to pull my dork out of her twat, where it still was at the time, her hands were down there, like sixty, to grab hold of my dick and guide it right to the small door of its proposed new home.

"For me, this was not a first time something like this happened, each time with a different woman. Oh, not *exactly* that same way. I mean, they always didn't ask me to fuck their ass while my cock was still hard and sticky with cum up their satisfied twats. Nor did they always get *so* carried away that they pulled my cock to their assholes for me. However, I have found that there are increasing numbers of women and men who want anal stimulation.

"While my fucking of her cunt had been a relatively mechanical operation on my part—more like a scientist conducting an experiment wherein the objective was to give pleasure—the minute my dick was positioned at her asshole, it became an entirely new ballgame.

"All mechanical aspects of my previous fuck disappeared and were replaced by spontaneous enthusiasm and *go-to-it-ness*.

"After I fucked my cock in and up her asshole, I did *try* to maintain control, did *try* to observe, and did *try* to program myself to give calculated responses. But passion, posthaste, took over from reason.

"Her asshole was tight and was holding on for dear life to the entire length of my submerged pecker. I felt pleasures swelling non-stop within my body. The more I manipulated my dick within her bunghole, the higher plateaus of pleasure I reached.

"She seemed to be appreciating her ass-fuck almost as much, if not more so, as the front-door screw I'd just delivered. She was groaning, moaning, and her thighs were clamping my waist. My balls frantically banged her ass as I pumped her.

"Jesus, my cock was harder than it had ever been up her cunt. My balls moved in my scrotal bag, like two cats fighting; they were busily in the process of making semen for my second coming.

"I dragged my tongue over her sweaty cheeks and neck and tits, tasting the saltiness of her sweat—and enjoying the taste. I revolved my hips, stirring my prick within her gripping a-hole. Again, I groaned with genuine enjoyment.

"My breathing became decidedly erratic, and heat built up inside my guts.

"I gave her some long and powerful strokes. Each thrust buried my dick to its full depth. Each withdrawal pulled out my cock until only its mere head was engulfed by her rubber-band sphincter.

"My belly dragged across the hair of her cunt and turned wet with ooze that was partly her natural cunt juice and partly the cum with which I'd so recently basted that front hole of hers.

"Where I'd enjoyed total brain-control the whole time I was screwing her pussy, I suddenly realized that my cock was taking over. No matter how much I fought to make it otherwise, it was a losing battle. While fucking her asshole, I turned into just another rutting beast. I derived just too much pleasure, each time my cock was sucked into that smelly hole of hers, to want anything but more of the same.

"This ass-fuck was doomed to be shorter-lived than my preceding screw of her snatch. For even though my cock had already blasted once (up her cunt), I was so turned on by my prick up her asshole that I could feel my guts tying themselves into tight knots in preparation for hasty climax.

"My hips picked up speed. My cock's strokes became shorter. I became acutely aware of each and every inch of my priming erection slipping within her bowels.

"She writhed sensuously beneath me. She arched her back, ground her butt up into me, and groaned out her appreciation.

"Waves of ecstasy washed over me. I felt on the verge of drowning.

"My nuts ballooned all the larger with their increasing reservoirs of cum; she hand-squeezed my gone-hyper-sensitive testicles.

"Do you want to know what happened next? Well, I suddenly and unexpectedly got *my* butt filled with all the lovely inches of my cousin Adrian's erection. The surprise of it happening, so without warning, and the wonder of all his hard meat just gliding on into me, just like that—into my asshole and over my prostate—sent this boy off into the wild-blue yonder. While Adrian stuck my ass, I let go with a wad up that gal's asshole that she must have felt all of the way to the roots of her hair.

"God knows when Adrian had arrived on the scene. The girl and I had been so caught up in our fun and games that neither of us heard him arrive. He told me later that he'd stood in the doorway and watched us for a long time before he'd even decided to join in. I'm sure as hell glad that he decided to join in, and bring along his big hard dick, let me tell you. So, for that matter, was the girl; it would be one hell of a long time, if ever, before she forgot *that* night.

"The three of us fucked, sucked, ate ass, bung-screwed, cunt-licked, and did each other over, every which way from Sunday, until the sun was long up in the morning.

"That was one wonderful mother-fuckin' evening, let me tell you. But then living with my cousin Adrian is *never* dull."

ANAL COUSINS, BY WILLIAM MALTESE

V.

CONCLUSION

DR. SIGMUND FREUD states in his *Basic Writings*:

> It is loathing which stamps as a perversion the use of the anus as a sexual aim. But it should not be interpreted as espousing a course when I observe that the basis of this loathing—namely, that this part of the body serves for the excretion and comes into contact with the loathsome excrement—is no more plausible than the basis which hysterical girls have for the disgust which they entertain for the male genital because it serves for urination.

Freud goes on to say:

> ...the anal zone is, through its position, adapted to produce an anaclisis of sexuality to other functions of the body. It should be assumed that the

erogenous significance of this region of
the body was originally very strong.
Through psychoanalysis one finds, not
without surprise, the many transforma-
tions that normally take place in the
sexual excitation emanating from here,
and this zone often retains for life a
considerable fragment of genital irrita-
bility....

This book has given illustrations of several per-
sons who have involved themselves in anal-oriented
sex and who have survived their encounters with
apparently no real harm done.

The case histories have illustrated a few of the
reasons why people may turn to anal sex rather than
participate in the more normally accepted forms of
coitus. These reasons range from fear of pregnancy,
need to preserve virginity, acts of rebellion, and
homosexuality, to utilizing it as an attempted adjustment to a series of traumatic experiences. There
are undoubtedly many more reasons why people
turn to anal sex exclusively, or use it as a comple-
ment to the more accepted forms of sexual congress.

In these days of more and more "sexual liberal-
ism," more and more people seem to be finally doing things which they judge right *for themselves*.

Says Allan Fromme in *Ability to Love*:

By a well-adjusted person, a normal person, we mean one who has
achieved a reasonable relationship between his needs and abilities on the one

hand and his social opportunities...on the other.

The normal person is free to propose and pursue rational goals. By 'rational' in this context we mean goals that are the product of thought....

It is interesting to note how easily these people rationalized their participation not only in anal sex but in incestuous relationships. In every case, the incestuous implications were recognized by the participants. In each case, the incestuous implications were considered only minor obstacles, if obstacles at all, and were quickly dealt with and/or passed over.

Is society, then, beginning to become more accepting of incest as well as anal sex? The answer can only come through more interviews, taped conversations, examinations of more case histories like those included within this work.

Perhaps, under certain circumstances, incest today is acceptable. Perhaps, under certain circumstances, anal sex today is acceptable. Perhaps, under certain circumstances today they are both to be preferred to alternatives available at the time.

Havelock Ellis, in his classic *Psychology of Sex*, says:

In determining what is natural for man, we are not entitled to consider the practice of the animals belonging to remote genera. We have to consider the general practice of the human species, which by no means shows so narrowly exclusive an aim in procreation.... We are quite justified in departing, if we think fit, from the habits of the lower races. Certainly, the sexual organs were developed for procreation, not for the sexual gratification of the individual; certainly also the hands were developed to serve nutrition, not to play on the piano or the violin. But if the individual can find joy and inspiration in using his organs for ends they were not made for, he is following a course of action which, whether or not we choose to call it 'natural,' is perfectly justifiable and moral.... Human art legitimately comes into human activities, but it introduces a real conflict with Nature.

Richard F. Hettlinger, in *Living with Sex: The Student's Dilemma*, states:

Instead of measuring our humanity by the refined dualism of the medieval monastery or the statistical uniformity of the average man, we must consider its unique qualities and fulfill our sexuality within this context.

BIBLIOGRAPHY

Bross, Barbara; Gilbey, Jay. COMPLETE SEXUAL FULFILLMENT. New York: Signet Books, 1968.

Ellis, Albert. SEX WITHOUT GUILT. New York: Grove Press, Inc., 1965.

Ellis, Havelock. PSYCHOLOGY OF SEX. London: Pan Books, 1959.

Freud, Sigmund. BASIC WRITINGS. New York: Random House, Inc., 1938.

Fromme, Allan. ABILITY TO LOVE. New York: Pocket Books, Inc., 1965.

Goldenson, Robert. THE ENCYCLOPEDIA OF HUMAN BEHAVIOR. Garden City: Doubleday and Company, Inc., 1970.

Hegeler, Inge; Hegeler, Sten. ABZ OF LOVE. New York: Medical Press of New York, 1963.

Hettlinger, Richard F. LIVING WITH SEX: THE STUDENT'S DILEMMA. New York: The Seabury Press, 1967.

Horney, Karen. THE NEUROTIC PERSONALITY OF OUR TIME. New York: W.W. Norton and Co., Inc., 1937.

"J". THE SENSUOUS WOMAN. New York: Lyle Stuart, Inc., 1969.

Kinsey, A.C.; Pomeroy, W.B.; Martin, C.E. SEXUAL BEHAVIOR IN THE HUMAN MALE. Philadelphia: W.B. Saunders, Co., 1948.

McCary, James L. HUMAN SEXUALITY. New York: Van Nostrand-Reinhold Books, 1967.

Reuben, David. WHAT YOU ALWAYS WANTED TO KNOW ABOUT SEX. New York: David McKay Co., 1969.

Thorpe, Louis P.; Katz, Barney. THE PSYCHOLOGY OF ABNORMAL BEHAVIOR. New York: The Ronald Press Company, 1961.

Valensin, Georges. SEX FROM A TO Z. New York: Berkley Medallion Books, 1969.

Wells, John Warren. COMPARATIVE SEX TECHNIQUES. New York: Lancer Books, Inc., 1968.

White, Robert W. THE ABNORMAL PERSONALITY. New York: The Ronald Press Co., 1964.

ABOUT THE AUTHOR

WILLIAM MALTESE was born in the Pacific North-west. He has a B.A. in Marketing/Advertising and spent an honorable tour of duty in the U.S. Army, achieving the rank of E-5.

He started his authorial career writing for the men's pulp magazines and has since penned more than 150 books, both fiction and nonfiction. According to queerhorror.com, this included the first gay werewolf novel ever published. He also has written a number of bestselling women's romances for houses such as Harlequin and Carousel, including the internationally acclaimed Harlequin SuperRomance #2 (*Love's Emerald Flame*), which is being reprinted by Wildside Press along with many of his other novels.

He encourages his fans to visit his websites:

www.williammaltese.com
www.myspace.com/williammaltese